'This is a ve
interview,

'I'm an unorthodox man.' The
Celena's whole body tingling.

'Do you always use your sex appeal to get
what you want?' She kept her voice cool.

Luciano's mouth twitched at the corners. 'Was
that what I was doing? I wasn't aware of the
fact. However, if I'm managing to persuade
you that you'd be doing both yourself and me
a favour by taking this job, then it's not a bad
thing. . .'

Born in the industrial heart of England, **Margaret Mayo** now lives with her husband in a pretty Staffordshire canalside village. Once a secretary, she turned her hand to writing her books both at home and in exotic locations, combining her hobby of photography with her research.

Recent titles by the same author:

STOLEN FEELINGS

POWERFUL PERSUASION

BY
MARGARET MAYO

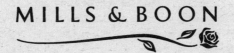

MILLS & BOON

*MILLS & BOON and the Rose Device
are trademarks of the publisher.
Harlequin Mills & Boon Limited,
Eton House, 18–24 Paradise Road, Richmond, Surrey TW9 1SR*

© Margaret Mayo 1996

ISBN 0 263 79844 5

*Set in 10 on 11 pt Linotron Times
01-9612-56971*

*Typeset in Great Britain by CentraCet, Cambridge
Made and printed in Great Britain*

CHAPTER ONE

CELENA'S heart missed a beat as she walked into the room. Quite what she had expected Luciano Segurini to look like she was not sure: certainly not quite so tall, or so imposing, *or so magnificently male!*

She had anticipated a powerful figure of a man, authority sitting easily on his shoulders, a man with massive self-confidence—he wouldn't have got where he was today without it—but she had not envisaged someone whose very presence filled the room with raw sexuality; it was almost tangible.

He had shiny, jet-black hair, side-parted and swept back, a square chin and hollow cheeks which made him look somewhat gaunt, a long, straight nose, slightly flared at the nostrils, and a full lower lip. He was not conventionally handsome and yet the combination of all these features made him lethally attractive.

'Miss Coulsden.' His dark, velvet-brown eyes looked unnervingly into hers and he took her hand in a grip that threatened to crush every bone. It lasted, Celena felt, for much longer than was necessary, and afterwards it was difficult to restrain herself from rubbing life back into her tingling fingers.

'Please, sit down.'

With a name like Segurini she had expected a foreign accent; instead he spoke perfect English, in a deep, gravelly voice that seduced her nerve-endings and sent dangerous waves of awareness through her body. She could not understand what was happening. She had come here for a job interview and instead was feeling disturbingly erotic sensations.

After her engagement to Andrew Holmes had ended so disastrously she had been careful never to let any man close again. She instinctively distrusted the whole male sex and had built a defensive wall around herself, cutting out of her life anyone who came close to dislodging even one brick. People said she had changed after Andrew and maybe she had, but it was her way of dealing with it.

And when her parents had died in a skiing accident a couple of years later Celena had been glad she had not married him. Her younger sister, Davina, was at boarding-school and Celena determined to keep her there. Andrew would most definitely not have approved; he had had very firm views about paying for an education. He'd considered it a complete waste of money when there were perfectly adequate state schools. The fact that Celena herself had been to boarding-school had always been a bone of contention between them.

It was because of Andrew that she could not understand her chemical reaction to this man now, this stimulus from him to her. It made a mockery of her every effort to school herself against reacting to any man and she felt quite sure that he too would be horrified if he knew what thoughts were surging through her mind.

She sat thankfully. 'Thank you.'

He waited until she was comfortable before seating himself behind a huge curved desk that was home to a battery of technological equipment. Any lesser man would have been dwarfed by it, but not Luciano Segurini. And when he tapped on a keyboard she noticed that he had very long fingers, square at the ends with well-manicured nails. Strong hands, strong fingers—no wonder they had almost pulverised her!

'Now, let me see.' It was almost as though he was talking to himself. 'Celena Coulsden—single, age twenty-eight, five A levels, a distinction in design and graphics at Brampton College, began work at—'

'Just a minute.' Celena stopped him with an agitated movement of her hand and a frown of incredulity. 'How did you gain all this information?' It was unbelievable. Why had he considered it necessary to check on her like this? What else did he know? Her dress-size? Her shoe-size? Her favourite perfume? She felt distinctly uneasy. There was definitely something going on here that she did not understand.

First of all she'd been offered a job right out of the blue when she hadn't even been looking for one, and now this amazing man was disclosing that he already had a very complete and very accurate file on her. Her heart raced again, through for a very different reason this time: she felt a deep sense of foreboding.

He smiled, showing very even, very white, very large teeth. If it was meant to reassure her it didn't. It was a wolfish smile; he was the predator and she was his prey!

Go careful, Lena, she told herself. This man is highly dangerous.

'There is nothing I cannot find out, Miss Coulsden— if I want to. There is nothing I cannot do.'

It was his unutterable confidence that astounded her. Had that been a threat? It had sounded ominous. She stood up, tall herself at five feet eight, and tossed back her shoulder-length auburn hair, her eyes a dark, stormy grey. 'I think we're wasting each other's time, Mr Segurini. I should not have come. I'm perfectly happy in the job I have, thank you very much.'

She was dressed in startling, vibrant red—a colour which should have clashed outrageously with her hair but which somehow looked exactly right. She slung her black leather shoulder bag into place and headed for the door, but his imperative, 'Wait!' made her halt before she was even halfway across the room.

Slowly Celena turned, brown eyes meeting grey, his faintly amused, her own hostile and defensive, her chin high. Her heart began to thud. It had to be the uniqueness of the situation, not the man himself, she decided fiercely.

'You are offended that I have already checked up on you?' His clerical grey suit sat easily on wide shoulders, complemented by a white silk shirt and a red and grey Paisley silk tie.

'As a matter of fact, yes I am,' she answered, and was appalled to hear how husky her voice sounded. She cleared her throat. 'I'm not even working for you and yet you have a dossier on me. I find that totally unacceptable.'

'I think you'll agree that in this day and age most people are on computer lists somewhere. It is surprising how much information is held by all sorts of people— your bank manager, for instance; he probably knows a lot more about you than you think.'

'Maybe,' she conceded with a shrug, 'but why you?'

He smiled—again the wolfish smile that sent shivers down her spine. 'Think about it, Miss Coulsden; I would hardly offer a job, especially such an important job, to someone I knew nothing about.'

'Agreed,' she said, wondering briefly what he meant by important. 'But how did you come by all this information? We have never met, have we? How did you know about me? Why do you want me in particular? I am sure there must be plenty of other copywriters who come up to the standard you require.'

He inclined his head thoughtfully to one side and pursed his lips. 'You have forged an excellent reputation for yourself. The ads you have handled have been some of the most successful run by your company.'

Celena was always modest about her success. She shrugged. 'I simply write the words.'

'But what words.' He looked at her approvingly.

She ignored the triggering of her senses.

'What I do not understand is why you have concentrated on that side of advertising when you have the talent for design.'

'I enjoy it more,' she said simply.

'And I want you on my team.' It was a dark declaration. 'There is nothing I cannot do.' His earlier words rang in Celena's ears. He wanted her and meant to have her—whether she wished it or not!

To begin with, when she had received Luciano Segurini's offer, she had felt flattered and surprised— yes, very surprised, shocked even, but intrigued also, and pleased that he thought her good enough to join Luse, one of England's top advertising agencies. It would be to her advantage, he'd said, which she'd taken to mean that he would be offering her a higher salary than she was getting now—and how useful that would be.

She had lain awake at night recently, wondering how she could afford Davina's next term's boarding-school fees. What money her parents had left had already been eaten up, although Davina did not know that, and Celena would have worked night and day rather than disclose this fact. Her sister was intensely happy at her school—it was the same one Celena herself had attended—and it could affect her whole education if she had to leave now.

Celena had inevitably wondered why Luciano Segurini had chosen her for this job, how he knew about her even, coming up with the deduction that most agencies kept an eye on their competitors. People talked; it was not inconceivable that he had heard about her.

He'd been right when he'd said that she had had a fair amount of success. In fact Hillier and Jones were extremely proud of her and it was doubtful whether they would let her go. She had not even told them that she was coming for this interview. It was curiosity alone that had led her here. And now, because of her astonishing reaction to this man, and because he already knew so much about her, she was beginning to wish that she had not been so tempted. It was an eerie feeling knowing that she had been checked on so thoroughly.

'I want you to work on the most important undertaking of my life.'

Celena looked at him with a questioning frown.

'You are the very person I have been looking for. You have exactly the right qualifications.'

'I would imagine,' she said tightly, 'that with the success your company has achieved over the years you already have a highly qualified team.'

'There is always room for improvement,' he told her.

'New blood, you mean. Have you been let down? Are you a man short, is that it?'

He gave a twisted smile that seemed to sit unhappily on his lips. 'Yes, I've been let down—badly, as it happens. Will you take the job, Celena?'

She hardly noticed the fact that he had used her first name. Her eyes were on his mouth, on that full, sensual bottom lip, and she wondered what it would be like to be kissed by this man.

When she realised that he appeared to be waiting for an answer she came to with a guilty start. 'I'm sorry, what did you say?'

'I'll offer you double whatever it is you're earning now.'

Her finely moulded brows rose. 'Take a look at your screen, Mr Segurini; I'm sure it will tell you *exactly* what my present salary is.'

He smiled his appreciation. 'As a matter of fact, yes,

it does. It also tells me that you do not have a current boyfriend. Why is that? You're a very beautiful lady, Celena; you're—'

Her eyes flashed. 'My private life has nothing to do with my business life. You have no right prying.' She wondered whether he knew about her sister as well, and about the struggle she had to make ends meet— whether he knew that the temptation to accept his offer would be very strong.

He grinned. 'Actually it was pure and simple conjecture. But—I assume from your outrage that I am right. And that is good, because I shall expect you to work long hours and I do not want an irate boyfriend breathing down my neck.'

'I've not yet said I'll take the job,' Celena snapped, annoyed that he had tricked her.

'You'd be foolish not to,' he said. 'You'll be set up for life.'

'Life, Mr Segurini?' she exploded. 'I'm not giving my life to you.'

'But you are interested?' A confident smile played about his lips.

'I have a contract which—'

'Which can easily be broken,' he insisted. 'In any case, I understand that Hillier and Jones have hit a bad patch; there are redundancies in the offing. You could soon find yourself out of a job altogether.'

Celena looked at him sharply and suspiciously. 'It's news to me.' She half suspected that he was making it up.

'But it's true,' he said, suddenly serious. 'What is your answer?'

She shook her head. 'I cannot possibly give you one now. I cannot make such an important decision without giving it considerable thought.'

His eyes were steady on hers. 'What is there to think about?'

'A lot of things. For instance, would I be working directly under you?'

'We're a team, Celena.' The predatory smile was back in place. 'We work together.'

It was no answer at all as far as she was concerned.

'Sit down,' he said. 'I'll ask my secretary to bring you in some coffee. I have someone to see; I'll be back in ten minutes.'

And that was all the time he was giving her! What would he do, she wondered, if she said no? Would he offer her even more money? It was already a ridiculously high salary, far more than she was worth, although she wouldn't argue about that, and it would be extremely useful. In fact his offer was a lifeline, especially if Hillier and Jones *were* going out of business. It both confused and stunned her that she had heard no rumours to this effect.

But her main problem was Luciano Segurini himself, or at least her reaction to him. It set alarm bells jangling in her head, so loud that they threatened to deafen her. There was a strong danger that he could infiltrate her defences almost without her being aware of it.

Unless she was worrying for nothing! She'd never had much to do with Howard Hillier, the head of her present company, so maybe she wouldn't see very much of this man either. It would be stupid to turn down such an exceptional offer simply because she was afraid of this charismatic man, afraid of what he might do to her emotions. And yet she could not help thinking that there was something else behind it, something he wasn't telling her, some other more devious reason than needing a good copywriter.

Ten minutes had never passed so quickly. The sparsely furnished and yet functional office had settled down when he'd left, but the instant he returned it was filled with crackling electricity—and Celena's mind was not made up.

'Well, Celena?'

For the first time she realised that he was addressing her by her first name and she was not sure that she liked the familiarity. Actually no one ever called her Celena—everyone used the shortened form, Lena.

Nor did he resume his seat; instead he sat on the edge of his desk facing her, hands supporting him on either side, long legs outstretched. He was so close that she could smell the discreet, expensive aftershave he wore and it added to the drugging of her senses. No man had ever affected her like this, not so suddenly, not so violently—not against her will! Not even Andrew whom she had thought that she loved.

There was a pain in her chest where her heart pounded, a tightening of her throat, and she looked up at him and felt frightened. 'I—I can't take this job, *Mr* Segurini.'

'And why not, *Celena*?' A smile curved his lips though it did not reach his eyes, revealing his displeasure at her refusal.

'I need to find out whether it's true what you say about Hillier and Jones.'

'And when you find it is, what excuse will you use then?'

Celena drew in a deep breath. 'It's all very irregular, Mr Segurini. I cannot help feeling suspicious.'

'Are you saying the extra money would not be useful?' His voice was deep and disconcerting, sending shivers down her spine and uneasy sensations to the pit of her stomach.

'I guess money is always useful,' she admitted, 'but it's not always the answer.' And why the hell was she procrastinating? Why didn't she jump in with both feet and take his offer? Lord, she was a fool.

He pushed himself away from the desk and moved to the back of her chair, resting his hands on it and lowering himself so that his mouth was close to her ear. 'You're an amazing woman, Celena Coulsden.'

The soft words vibrated through every limb, through every nerve. She knew what he was doing—he was using his sensuality, confident that he would get through to her this way.

Fear struck. Surely he hadn't guessed that she already felt an unnerving response? Surely she hadn't given herself away? No, she was confident that she hadn't. He was playing games, certain that he would come out on top.

She moved quickly, pushing herself to her feet, dodging away from him. 'This is a very unorthodox interview, Mr Segurini.'

'I'm an unorthodox man.' It was a low growl, coming from somewhere deep in his throat. It set Celena's whole body tingling.

'Do you always use your sex appeal to get what you want?' She kept her voice cool, her chin high. Since Andrew she had had plenty of practice at keeping the wolves at bay. She had a classically beautiful face with high cheekbones, almond-shaped eyes and a wide, generous mouth, and these combined with her willowy figure and her thick auburn hair made her the target of many men's attention. She had got used to fending off their advances and now she gave Luciano Segurini one of her most damning looks.

His mouth twitched at the corners. 'Was that what I was doing?'

'It looked very much like it to me,' she retorted crossly.

'I wasn't aware of the fact.'

'Really?' she asked disbelievingly.

'I think your imagination is working overtime,' he told her as he slid into the chair that she had vacated and put his feet up on the edge of the desk. 'However, if I'm getting through to you, if I'm managing to persuade you that you would be doing both yourself and me a favour by taking this job, then it's not a bad thing.' He folded his arms and looked totally relaxed.

Celena was not deceived; he was still in complete command of the situation, though she was glad of the few feet that were now between them, and more especially of the advantage his sitting down had given her. She looked at him coldly. 'You're not getting through to me. As a matter of fact your behaviour is convincing me that I would be making a fatal mistake in accepting your offer.'

He frowned and sprang to his feet, his movements fluid despite the anger that surged through him. 'My sincere apologies, *Miss* Coulsden. I thought the informality would help. Obviously I was wrong.' He returned to his side of the desk and stood looking at her, and there was nothing now on his face to suggest that this was anything other than a normal job interview.

'And you were wrong in assuming I would jump at this opportunity,' she declared fiercely. 'I think we have nothing further to say. Good morning, Mr Segurini.' And even the fact that she knew she would regret her hastiness later did not make her change her mind.

To her amazement he let her go; he let her walk out of the room without saying another word, and when she got back to her office and made a few discreet enquiries she discovered that every word Luciano Segurini had said was true. It looked as though she was going to be jobless and penniless and Davina would definitely have to pull out of her school. The thought both saddened and distressed her.

* * *

That evening when she got home from work there was an enormous bouquet of white roses awaiting her. She picked them up from the doorstep and looked curiously at the card.

> To the most amazing woman I have ever met. The offer is still open if you should change your mind. I will be in touch.

It was not signed—it did not have to be—and while Celina was relieved, financially, that she might be offered the job all over again she groaned inwardly at the thought that there could be another confrontation with the most amazing man *she* had ever met. So far she had told no one of her experience, having used the excuse of a dental appointment to cover her absence, and now she opened the door and moved inside.

When her parents had died she had sold their draughty Victorian house in Norfolk and moved nearer to London and her job, and this cosy mews house suited her very well. If it hadn't been for Davina's school fees she would have managed quite comfortably—as things stood it was a definite struggle.

She dropped the flowers on the kitchen worktop, contemplating whether to relegate them to the dustbin. If she dared put them in a vase they would be a constant reminder of the man who had had such a profound effect on her in such a short space of time. She took a shower and slipped into a comfortable jade-green silk jumpsuit.

She prepared her evening meal—cold chicken left over from Sunday, with a green salad and new potatoes—and still the sweet-smelling roses lay where she had left them. She had just finished eating when the doorbell rang. As she was constantly being pestered by callers Celena was tempted not to answer—until it rang again and whoever it was kept a finger on the button.

Normally before opening the door Celena made sure that the safety chain was in place. On this occasion, however, she snatched it open without even thinking, intent on giving whoever it was a piece of her mind. Her mouth fell open. 'Mr Segurini! What are you doing here?'

He smiled unnervingly. 'I'm checking that my flowers arrived safely.'

Celena's eyes were guarded. 'A phone call would have sufficed. And yes, they have, thank you very much, though I can't think why you sent them.'

'I hope you like white roses.' His thickly fringed eyes made a slow and thorough appraisal of her body, starting at the tip of her pink-painted toenails, rising slowly, pausing fractionally on her breasts, and again on her mouth, then coming to a complete halt when they reached her eyes.

Celena felt breathless. 'Yes,' she whispered. They were her favourite, though he couldn't have known that.

'It's a pity that when one orders flowers one never actually gets to see them.'

'If you're after an invite into my house then you're out of luck.' She desperately tried to quell the surging of her senses. He had changed into a pair of lightweight blue trousers and a matching cashmere sweater, the casual clothes emphasising his hard-muscled body, making him an even more dangerous adversary. Her mind might tell her that he was not to be trusted, but her body certainly had no such reservations.

'I thought perhaps we could go out for a drink, get to know each other better, discuss my offer in more detail.' He smiled as he spoke, his brown eyes still intent on hers.

The audacity of the man! Celena's heart leapt but she

made herself frown, saying crossly, 'Don't you ever take no for an answer?'

'Not if I really want something.'

'And you want me?' It was the wrong thing to have said; she felt a flush coming to her cheeks, which was insane—she hadn't blushed in years. Celena decided to rephrase her question. 'I mean, you want me to work for you?'

His lips twitched as he recognised her discomfiture. 'You're perfect for the job.'

'I think there's more to it,' she retorted.

He frowned. 'What ever gave you that idea?'

'Your insistence, for one thing.'

'And for another?'

'Feminine intuition.' Her tone was cool. She had herself in control now.

He smiled. 'Ah, that.'

'Yes, that,' she snapped. 'Are you denying that I am right?'

'It's an interesting theory. How about we go out and discuss it?'

Celena let out an impatient sigh. 'I don't want to go out. I've had a hell of a day, with no thanks to you; I planned on an early night.'

He shot a glance at his watch—an expensive gold affair. Cartier probably, she decided, seeing the Roman numerals on its face. Everything about this man spelt wealth, and he seemed to think that it could get him whatever he wanted. She had no doubt that he intended to offer her an even higher salary.

'It's early yet—only a little after eight,' he said. 'Perhaps we could talk here? I promise to take up no more than an hour of your time.'

She felt a fresh surge of apprehension. 'I never allow strangers into my house.'

Thick brows lifted. 'I don't think we're entirely

strangers, and I promise you, Miss Coulsden, that my intentions are strictly honourable.' He chuckled as he said it. 'An old-fashioned turn of phrase. Let me put it another way. I have no designs on your body, beautiful though it is. You'll be perfectly safe.'

And Celena surprised herself by believing him. She found him dangerous in many ways, but felt instinctively that she could accept his word on this occasion. 'Very well.' She stepped back reluctantly. 'Though I promise you you'll be wasting your time; I never change my mind once it is made up.'

His lips quirked. 'And I never accept no for an answer. An impasse, no less. It will be interesting to see who wins.'

The character of the house changed as he stepped inside. It had always had a relaxed, comfortable feeling, but the instant this man entered the whole atmosphere became charged—as it had in his office! It was going to be a difficult meeting, Celena decided.

She led him down the hallway to her sitting room at the back, which overlooked a pleasant courtyard which she had filled with tubs and containers growing a profusion of colourful plants and climbing shrubs, making the small area look almost Mediterranean.

'Please sit down.' She indicated a dumpy armchair that she had recovered in rust linen, but sat on the opposite side of the room herself on a straight wooden chair with her back to the French windows. It put him at a disadvantage because the low evening sunlight slanted right into his eyes.

She had reckoned without his guessing her tactics. He got up and smiled—that wolfish smile which hinted that he was in complete control. 'You take the comfortable chair.'

He held out a hand and she had no choice, but she ignored his offer of help, pulling the curtains slightly before she sat down. But not enough. The sun still caught the chair and made her squint as she looked at him.

'The hot spot?' he queried. 'Good try, Miss Coulsden, but I prefer to be the one in control.'

She said nothing, hiding her embarrassment, looking at him with her lips clamped together, her grey eyes stormy. 'OK, make your offer.'

Their eyes met and held for several long, suspenseful seconds—seconds during which Celena's heart catapulted once again with violent emotion.

'I think,' he said, his tone low and meaningful, 'that first of all we ought to analyse your motives for refusing.'

She lifted one eyebrow. 'Analyse? There is nothing to analyse.'

'No?' he asked sceptically. 'No one except the very rich wouldn't like to earn more money.'

Her eyes flashed. 'And you're one of that élite band, thinking that your money can buy anything you've set your heart on. Let me tell you this, Mr Segurini—I refuse to be bought. Didn't I make myself clear?'

'Did you check on the situation with your present employers?'

She inclined her head. 'You were right,' she admitted grudgingly.

'And you have a mortgage on this house?'

'I don't see that that is any business of yours,' she retorted. He probably knew anyway; it was very likely one of the pieces of information stored in his computer system. Her parents' house hadn't fetched all that much, and property here was so much dearer, so yes, she did have a mortgage.

'And then, of course,' he said with a slow, knowing smile as he delivered his pièce de résistance, 'there are your sister's school fees. It must be quite a struggle for you, Celena.'

Celena gasped, even though she knew she ought not to be surprised, and jumped to her feet, moving so that the sun was not glaring into her eyes. 'Get out of here, you swine. You have no right prying into—'

'You're even more beautiful when you're angry,' he cut in softly. 'It amazes me that some man hasn't snapped you up before now. You need the job, Celena; why don't you take it?'

He was right—she did need it; she could not afford to turn him down a second time. But there was still defiance in her eyes. 'Only if you triple my present salary,' she declared, chin jutting.

A wide smile softened the harsh contours of his face; white teeth gleamed. 'Done.' He stood too and held out his hand and Celena was compelled to take it. 'I knew you would come to your senses. Everyone has their price.'

His grip pulverised her hand, but more shocking than that were the waves of electricity that ran through her—the chemical reaction that she had felt in his office but which was much stronger here. Please God, don't let our paths cross too often, she prayed silently.

CHAPTER TWO

ONE month later Celena began working for Luse and for the first week and a half, much to her relief, she saw nothing of Luciano, though his name was on everyone's lips. Luciano this, Luciano that, Luciano wants, Luciano would like, et cetera, et cetera. And Luciano got!

She was also quizzed tirelessly as to how she had got her job. No one had left; there had been no real vacancy. It was apparently a made-up job, and one that puzzled everyone else as much as Celena. A second bouquet of white roses had arrived—this time the card had simply read 'Thank you'.

And then came the summons to the big man's office. To her annoyance Celena felt her heart pounding long before she reached the end of the corridor which took her to his room. She paused a moment outside to regain her equilibrium and was standing there breathing deeply when the door was suddenly yanked opened.

'What are you doing, Miss Coulsden?' Luciano Segurini asked with considerable amusement. 'Plucking up courage to face the lion in his den?'

He was so very near the mark that to save herself embarrassment she said, 'Naturally. You're held in very high esteem, Mr Segurini. A call to your sanctum is not to be treated lightly. What is it—am I getting the sack, or a raise?'

His lips quirked as he motioned her inside. 'Very few of my employees would dare to speak to me like that.'

'Really?' She allowed a faint frown. 'Didn't you tell me, just after I accepted this job, that you're one big happy family here? No distinction between the classes,

22

so to speak? If that is the case I see no reason why I can't say what I like.' As he had been ready to go to any lengths to employ her she had no fear of dismissal.

'No matter.' He motioned her to sit down, settling himself behind his huge desk as he had on that first occasion. And now, as then, Celena felt her skin tingle, felt the enormous pull of his magnetism, and puzzled anew at her unexpected and uncharacteristic response.

'Have you any immediate plans, Celena?'

She frowned faintly, not altogether sure that she understood.

'I mean personal ones. Holidays, that sort of thing.' His tone was crisp and professional and it was a relief to hear him talking like this.

'No.' She resisted the temptation to say she was sure that he knew anyway, that he had everything on computer down to the birthmark on her left thigh. He probably even knew what her bank balance was.

'Good, because I want you to accompany me to Sicily.'

'Sicily?' she repeated in amazement.

'Yes, my home country.'

'And for what reason am I to accompany you?' Alarm bells sounded once again in her head—extra loud ones this time.

'Purely business, of course. I handle quite a lot of advertising over there.'

'And why do you need me?'

'Isn't that clear?' he asked sharply, as though she was stupid for missing the point. 'You're doubly qualified. It will save both time and money if you can come up with ideas on the spot.'

She eyed him guardedly. 'And this is what you had in mind right from the offset?'

He inclined his head.

'Why didn't you say so?'

'Would you have agreed to work for me, knowing I was going to whisk you off abroad?' He tapped a pencil on his thumbnail and watched her closely.

Celena smiled faintly. 'Maybe not. On the other hand I might have seen it as an exciting opportunity.'

'So you are happy about accompanying me?'

She saw no point in arguing: he would undoubtedly get his own way in the end. 'So long as it is strictly business.'

'You have my word,' he said.

'How long will we be away?'

He shrugged. 'A day or two—just long enough to tie things up.'

The flight took two and a half hours. They booked into a hotel in Palermo, and over dinner Luciano surprised her by talking about his childhood.

'Families here are very close knit, as you probably know. My mother died when I was four and I was brought up by my maternal grandparents—with a great deal of well-intentioned interference from my great-grandmother. Although neither my father nor my grandparents are alive now, Bisnonna still is, bless her heart. She will be ninety-three this year.'

He sounded very fond of her and Celena felt envious for a moment as she had no grandparents of her own, both sets having died when she was very young, before Davina had even been born.

'I went to England to finish my education at Oxford,' he went on, 'and liked your country so much that I made it my home. Naturally I still come back here several times a year; my family would never forgive me if I didn't.'

'You have brothers and sisters?' she asked.

He inclined his head. 'Two brothers and a sister:

Gabriella—she is the youngest; Paolo is next, then Filippo. You will meet them tomorrow.'

Celena frowned sharply. 'We are visiting your family?'

'Naturally. I couldn't possibly come to Sicily and not see them.'

'You told me it was purely a business trip,' she said accusingly.

His lips curved. 'And what is wrong with combining business with pleasure? Treat the break as an added bonus, Celena.'

Some bonus, she thought. 'Are they married, your brothers and sister?'

'All of them.'

'So why aren't you?' It was a question she ought not to have asked; it was too intrusive, considering they were employer and employee, and the sudden harshness of his face confirmed it. 'I'm sorry,' she said quickly. 'Forget I said that. This is a very good bolognese.'

'And so it should be.' His face relaxed. 'But wait until you taste *our* bolognese. It is a very special family recipe. It is *meraviglioso*.'

There was obviously some reason why he hadn't married and she wondered what it was. She guessed him to be somewhere in his mid-thirties and found it strange that he was still a bachelor. He was most eligible so why had no one snapped him up? The fault had to lie with him. Maybe his work took up too much of his time. Maybe he'd had a bad experience. Maybe, maybe— there could be a thousand and one explanations.

In bed that night, in her hotel room next to Luciano's, Celena could not rid her mind of him. He had to be the most intriguing man she had ever met—visually excit-

ing, physically stimulating, disgustingly rich—everything a girl could wish for.

It disturbed her that Luciano had made such a strong
impact, that he was infiltrating her defences so easily.
After the numbing discovery that Andrew was seeing
another woman behind her back she had thought herself immune to this sort of thing. This coupled with the
fact that the girl had been her best friend had made her
vow never to trust anyone again. She had thrown herself
wholeheartedly into her career and no one since had
managed to arouse any sort of feeling within her. She
was even nicknamed 'the ice-woman' among her
contemporaries.

The short flight from England in Luciano's private jet
had been an experience in itself. Not only had she been
impressed that he had his own plane, and that it was
fitted out to very high standards with a comfortable
lounge and a fully equipped office, she had also been
overwhelmed by the strength of his personality.

Each time they met the air tingled, but in the close
confines of his Lear jet Celena had felt it even more
strongly. She had experienced great difficulty in breathing, as though there had been no air in the cabin. He'd
filled the whole space with his presence, and although
he had busied himself at his computer, keeping in touch
with everything that was going on in his business world,
she had been unable to ignore him.

And now, even though a brick wall divided them, she
could still feel him, still sense the hidden power he
wielded over her. It troubled her deeply; he was most
definitely a force to be reckoned with.

Very little sleep and an early morning call, as well as
her uneasiness where Luciano was concerned, made
Celena irritable, and when she met him at the breakfast
table she barely smiled.

'Are you not feeling well?' he asked, looking fresh and vital in a white shirt and dark linen trousers, the inevitable aftershave faintly tormenting her, black hair still damp from his shower.

'I have a headache.' It was a lie but the best excuse she could come up with. She couldn't very well say, I lay awake all night thinking about you. It confused even her.

He had been in her life for six weeks, they had made contact on only three occasions before coming out here, and yet he had completely taken over her mind. It was crazy. At least he had kept his word and made no advances—*yet*! She had been sure to lock her door last night.

'Are you prone to headaches?' he asked sharply. 'Do you suffer from migraine?'

Celena shook her head.

'Then I guess it's just the travelling and the change. Take a couple of aspirin; you'll soon feel better.'

'What are our plans for today?' she asked. She felt uncomfortable about being introduced to his relatives. Would they believe the strictly business scenario? Or would they think she was his current girlfriend? Did he frequently take girls home?

She dismissed the thought immediately. He had told her that he had come from a very old Sicilian family, an aristocratic family no less, with old-fashioned views on girlfriends and marriage. He would hardly give the impression of being a philanderer.

'This morning, business,' he answered, his chin lifted in one of his unconscious arrogant gestures. 'This afternoon we will visit my family.' He watched her closely as he spoke, saw her sudden tension. 'Do not worry, Celena; they will love you.'

She frowned. *Love* her! It was an odd expression. Why would they love a business associate? All along she had felt nervous about the whole thing—about the unexpected job offer, the unreal salary, and finally this trip to Sicily. Had she been right to worry? 'Is there something you haven't told me, Mr Segurini?'

'Luciano, please,' he said.

'Why?' Her grey eyes were as troubled as a storm-tossed sea.

'Why what?' he asked with a sudden frown.

'Why should I call you Luciano when you are the owner of the company that employs me? I think it would be wrong to be on first-name terms when I am the very newest member of your team, especially as this is a business trip.'

'Both business and pleasure,' he told her. 'It is always a pleasure to be with my family.'

'And always a pleasure to take a girl with you?' she asked sharply.

'No.' He paused a moment, seeming to be deep in thought. 'I have never taken a girl home.'

At least that answered one question. 'You've never been serious about anyone?'

A muscle moved in his jaw. 'Yes, I have been serious, but it didn't work out. I'd rather not discuss it. Have you finished? I want to make an early start.'

Celena realised that she had unwittingly hit a raw nerve, and although she was curious she knew it would be unwise to press the issue. Perhaps later, when she got to know him better, she might find out about this girl who had had such a profound effect on him. She was obviously the reason why he had never married.

Their appointment was with a well-known car-manufacturing company, and it was an exciting brief; Celena felt honoured that she had been asked to take part.

One other thing in her favour was that she spoke Italian—no doubt Luciano had known that as well when he'd invited her to take the job, she thought drily, and had been what he'd meant when he'd said she was doubly qualified—and even though the Sicilian dialect was different she was still able to understand, and the Sicilians themselves were impressed with her knowledge of their language. All in all she made a very big hit with them.

Afterwards they had lunch in a restaurant on the outskirts of Palermo and Luciano praised her warmly, but he did not linger; he was clearly anxious to see his family, and in particular his great-grandmother. He spoke of her constantly and it was very evident that there was a close bond between them.

He took the *autostrada* east along the coast, driving for about fifty miles before turning south through the centre of the island. The mountains were high and dramatic, river valleys cutting deeply into the landscape. The highway strode along the valley of the Hymera River, following the base of the Madonie Mountains, eventually arriving at the fortress town of Enna with its castle and its legend of Demeter and Persephone.

Finally Luciano stopped in front of an old *palazzo* on the outskirts of the town. Celena looked in wonder at the large, magnificent stone mansion with its arches and pillars and west wings and east wings and goodness knew what else. It had once, obviously, been very beautiful but now had a neglected air, as though no one bothered any more. Nevertheless she was extremely impressed. She had not envisaged anything as grand as this.

The grilled door swung slowly open as they approached, creaking on its hinges, and a young woman dressed in black smiled shyly at Luciano and curiously at Celena.

'*Buon giorno*, Francesca,' he said, and, still speaking

in his native language, added, 'My great-grandmother is expecting us?'

Francesca nodded, her smile widening, and she was obviously in complete awe of Luciano.

After introducing Celena he led her up an impressive, wide curving staircase. At the top was a stained-glass window through which the sun cast a myriad different colours. It was like walking into fairyland.

Along a red-carpeted corridor they went, through a door, and down another passage, all with ornate plaster-work and beautiful crystal chandeliers. A heavy wooden door faced them. Luciano knocked, and even he did not enter without permission.

'*Avanti!*'

Celena had expected a quiet, quavering voice, not this strong, authoritative one. She glanced questioningly at Luciano but all he did was smile reassuringly as they entered the shaded room.

Great-grandmother Segurini was tiny, sitting upright on a red velvet chair, dressed all in black, with a square of black lace over her white hair. Dark eyes had sunk into their sockets many years ago yet they held an imperiousness that told that she was still the undisputed matriarch of the family. They brightened when she saw her great-grandson and he moved swiftly across the room to kiss her cheek and give her a bear-like hug.

'You are here at last,' she said in her native tongue. 'I have waited so long for your visit, Luciano. And this is Celena? Come closer, child; let me look at you.'

Celena obediently edged forward, surprised that Luciano had already mentioned her.

'Goodness, you are prettier than your photograph!' exclaimed the woman.

Photograph! What was she talking about? Celena frowned at Luciano but he shook his head and made a tiny gesture with his hand for her to say nothing. She decided that any photograph must have been of his previous girlfriend and he wanted to save his great-grandmother embarrassment by keeping quiet. She and the girlfriend were obviously very similar in appearance for his great-grandmother to have made this mistake.

Celena's eyes had grown accustomed to the dimness now and she was able to see Giacoma Segurini more clearly. Thin, gnarled fingers were heavily adorned with diamonds and garnets, as were her throat and ears. She sat like a queen on her throne—and Celena had no doubt that this was how the family regarded her. But despite her upright bearing and her imperious air she looked pale and frail, as though her hold on life was very tenuous.

The old lady held out her hands and Celena took them and was given a kiss on each cheek. 'Luciano has chosen well,' she said, smiling happily. 'Everyone is very anxious to meet you.'

'But I'm not who you—' Celena began, anxious to set the matter straight. Out of the corner of her eye she saw Luciano stiffen, but she did not care. It was wrong of him to deceive his great-grandmother. Why couldn't he tell her the truth, for heaven's sake? But the old woman totally ignored Celena's attempt to speak.

'He has told you, I expect, that he is my eldest and most favourite great-grandchild?'

'Yes,' she admitted huskily. 'But I really must—'

'He has disappointed me, however, by not getting married before now. Thirty-seven!' She tutted as though scandalised. 'My own husband was twenty-two when I married him; I was twenty. When he was Luciano's age our eldest was already fourteen, and we had three other children besides. How old are you, Celena?'

'Twenty-eight,' she answered reluctantly. It was quite

obvious that she was not going to be given the chance to speak.

Again the old woman tutted. 'You people today, what is wrong with you? Where is all the love and romance gone? You work, work, work. You spend all your lives working instead of bringing up a family. I do not understand.'

'Things have changed, Bisnonna,' said Luciano.

The woman spread her hands expansively. 'Maybe, but I do not like it. I do not approve. At least now you have come to your senses and you have chosen a beautiful girl. Leave us alone, Luciano; I would like to talk with her.'

'Not now, Bisnonna,' he said soothingly, much to Celena's dismay. It would have been the ideal opportunity to tell this quite remarkable old lady exactly who she was. 'We were up early; we've had a busy day; Celena needs to rest.'

'Then later,' announced the woman regally.

Once outside the room Celena turned furiously on Luciano. 'What sort of game are you playing, letting your great-grandmother think that I am your girlfriend?'

'It is just a little deception,' he answered easily—too easily, Celena thought. 'It will do no harm.'

'I don't agree,' she retorted. 'The woman is in her element. How is she going to feel when she discovers that I'm nothing more than an employee? She looks so frail and ill that the shock will probably kill her.'

'Then perhaps we should say nothing.'

Celena's heart gave a warning thud and she looked at him warily. 'I trust you're not serious.'

'Perfectly,' he announced.

She shook her head. 'This is the most ridiculous thing I have ever heard. I will not be a part of it; I insist that you tell her, right now.'

'I cannot do that, Celena.' His brown eyes were steady on hers.

'Then I will tell her myself,' she declared firmly, and took a step back towards the door.

'Oh, no, you won't.' Luciano grasped her arm and forcibly led her away from his great-grandmother's apartment, and he did not stop until he reached the privacy of a book-filled study on the ground floor. There he sat her down on a burgundy leather chesterfield and his expression was utterly ruthless as he stood over her. 'I want my whole family to accept that you are my girlfriend.'

Celena stilled. 'This isn't accidental, is it?' she asked in a frozen whisper. 'You've set me up. The job was nothing more than a decoy.' She had expected something, had known he would not pay her such a high salary for nothing—but she had certainly never anticipated being put into such an uncomfortable and undesirable position.

'I wouldn't exactly say that,' he said, still with the same implacable expression on his face. 'You're already an asset to the team—a very valuable asset. This is just some little thing I want you to do for me.'

'Little?' she queried tartly. 'I don't call living a lie a little thing. It's outrageous; I absolutely refuse.'

'You would hurt my great-grandmamma?' he asked, and managed to sound astonished. 'As you said yourself, the shock of discovering what I am trying to do would very likely finish her off. It was purely to make an old woman very happy that I came up with this idea.

'But why me?' she asked tightly.

'Because—' he sat down beside her and attempted to take her hands into his, but Celena snatched angrily away '—because of your likeness to Simone,' he said. 'It's uncanny.'

'The girl in the photograph?'

'Yes.'

'The girl you didn't want to talk about?'

'The very same.'

'I think I deserve an explanation,' said Celena, her chin high, her eyes cold.

He was quiet for a moment and then said softly, 'Six months ago I thought I was in love with Simone; she was everything I wanted in a woman—beautiful, kind, loving. I'd had girlfriends on and off over the years, naturally, but Simone was someone special.'

'So what happened?'

His eyes turned black—deep, empty pits that echoed a pain he kept deep in his heart. 'I slowly began to realise that I was wrong about her, that she was shallow and selfish and nothing like the girl I'd imagined her to be. But it was not until she ditched me for a man even richer than myself—an older man—much older—' his lips twisted in disgust '—that I knew I'd been conned. She was yet another fortune-hunter—and I've had my fair share of those. A very clever one, a very talented lady. It certainly taught me a thing or two. I shall most definitely never fall in love again. I intend to remain a bachelor to the end of my days.'

'You had a rough time,' agreed Celena, privately thinking that he must have been a fool not to see through this woman, 'but I still don't understand why I should masquerade as Simone. What's wrong with telling your family the truth?'

'Because,' he said slowly, 'they are expecting you.'

CHAPTER THREE

'Expecting me?' squeaked Celena. 'I don't understand.'

Luciano's mouth twisted wryly. 'I'd already told them I'd met a wonderful girl, and obviously they expected me to bring her on this visit. I couldn't possibly let my *bisnonna* down. She has been so excited ever since she found out that there was finally someone serious in my life.'

He must love his great-grandmother very dearly, thought Celena, to want to carry out this charade, and found it a surprising side to his character—one she had not expected. She warmed to him a little but was still not sure that she wanted to be a part of his devious plot.

'I can't see it working,' she said, shaking her head. 'They will surely sense that there is no love between us.'

'I'm expecting you to put on an act.' His voice went an octave lower, his brown eyes locking with hers, and triggered her senses in a way no one else had. Not even Andrew had managed to arouse her just by the tone of his voice.

'I couldn't; I couldn't do that,' she told him breathlessly.

'Am I repulsive to you?' It was a sudden, animal growl, attacking her defences, sending her whole body into panic.

'No.' Her answer came out as a yelp and she swallowed and tried again. 'No, you're not, but—we're strangers—we—I—couldn't possibly—' And then on a

35

stronger note she said, 'I wish you'd been straight with me.'

His dark brows rose. 'I could hardly go up to a stranger and ask her to pretend to be my future wife.'

'So you dreamt up the job, got me out here, and hoped that when I saw your great-grandmother I would agree to do what you want,' she accused him heatedly.

He inclined his head. 'That was the general idea. She's quite a person, isn't she?'

The thought that he'd had his eye on her for some time sent a shiver of unease down Celena's spine. She did not like to think that he had been observing her, talking about her, collecting his dossier on her while she had been in complete ignorance. She could not recollect ever having seen him before—and yet he knew about her! He had chosen her because of her startling resemblance to Simone.

Changing the direction of her thoughts, Celena tried to imagine what the pretence—if she agreed to it—would be like, what meeting the rest of the family would be like. 'I'm no actress,' she said, speaking her thoughts out loud. 'I'm not sure that I could carry it off, Mr Segurini.'

He gave a snort of anger. 'Will you call me Luciano, *please*? And of course you can; there's nothing to it. Just forget I'm your employer; think of me as a friend— a close friend. Do that and the rest will fall into place.'

Celena wondered whether he realised the enormity of his request. It was unreal, unfair, and yet she did not like to think of the old woman upstairs being hurt, possibly giving up her fragile hold on life after all these years of waiting and hoping for Luciano to find himself a bride. It would be on her conscience for the rest of her life if that happened. Surely it wouldn't hurt to go along with it for a day or two?

Also, if she did refuse, he could quite easily terminate

her employment. And where would that leave her? And Davina? Fourteen now, top of her class, with excellent prospects, her sister dreamt about becoming a doctor— it was her passion in life. How could she be selfish enough to squash those dreams?

She heaved a sigh and Luciano must have seen the acceptance in her eyes because he said, 'Is that a yes?'

'I just hope I don't regret it,' Celena muttered.

'You'll knock them flat,' he declared. 'And I think now might be a good time to seal our bargain. You might even call it a rehearsal.'

Celena had no idea what he was talking about until he closed the gap between them and drew her into the circle of his arms. She opened her mouth to protest, only to find it captured by a pair of sensual, warm lips— lips that coaxed and burned and turned her insides to fire.

The kiss seemed to last for ever, every nerve and pulse in Celena's body responding instantly and feverishly. It was with a supreme effort of will that she kept her feelings hidden, and when Luciano finally pulled away, saying, 'Now that wasn't so bad, was it?' she looked heatedly into his face.

'I think you took an enormous liberty.' And deep down inside she was devastated to think how vulnerable she had suddenly become, how difficult the next few days were going to be.

'At least I've proved that you don't find me totally abhorrent.' He smiled, satisfied, and sat back away from her.

Celena's eyes flashed. 'You had better not do it too often,' she declared fiercely.

His lips quirked. 'I'm a very tactile man, Celena.'

'Well, you'd better be untactile where I'm concerned,' she raged, 'or you might end up with egg on your face.' Insisting that he leave her alone was her only form of defence, the only way she could keep her traitorous feelings hidden.

'Don't let me down, Celena.' It was spoken softly but a warning nevertheless.

She swallowed hard. 'It's the most difficult thing I've ever been asked to do.'

'I agree it's unusual,' he said, 'but I don't think it will be difficult, and naturally I shall make it worth your while.'

Celena pushed herself angrily to her feet. 'Why does everything always come down to money? As far as I'm concerned it's all part of my job—I don't want paying extra for it. Being paid to be kissed by you makes me sound like a—'

He interrupted her swiftly, harshly, springing up also. 'You've made your point, Celena. It's just that I'm used to—'

'Paying for whatever you want,' she cut in sharply. 'I'm not impressed. Don't forget my name's not Simone. There are some things money can't buy, Luciano. Hell, I can't call you that—it's too much of a mouthful. I'll call you Luc.' She pronounced it Luke.

He shrugged. 'As you wish.'

'What's going to happen when I've served my purpose?' she asked bluntly. 'Will I get my marching orders?'

His eyes flickered impatiently. 'The job will be yours for as long as you want it.'

'A high price to pay for a few days of someone *pretending* to be your girlfriend,' she retorted scathingly.

'I happen to think you're worth it.' Anger darkened his face now. 'Enough of this conversation. Francesca will show you to your room. Tonight my whole family is dining with us. Please dress yourself accordingly.' He was every inch the Sicilian aristocrat in that moment— and Celena hated him.

Along miles of corridor Francesca took her, finally opening a door and showing Celena inside. When the girl offered to unpack Celena shook her head with an apologetic smile. 'Thank you, but it won't be necessary; I haven't much.' And certainly nothing glamorous enough for a grand dinner with the Segurinis!

It was a large, high-ceilinged room with yet more ornate plasterwork and beautiful old furniture. The bare wooden floor was highly polished with a cotton rug either side of the bed. Furnished in muted shades of blue, it was pleasant and relaxing, though Celena was far too uptight to appreciate this fact.

The house was high on the mountainside and the tall, deep windows, with their stone balustrades, gave stunning panoramic views over the island. In the distance she could see Mount Etna and, to one side, the blue of the ocean, with drifts of colour from wild flowers on the hillside.

She sat for long moments staring out, thinking over the commitment she had made. Everything had conspired to make her say yes—Giacoma's obvious ill health, Davina's school fees, her own fear of being jobless. Everything. All she could hope was that she wouldn't live to regret it.

Eventually she took a shower in the adjoining bathroom, and then pulled on a pale green silk shirtwaister that she had packed in case they had any business dinners. It wasn't exactly what she would have chosen for the occasion confronting her now, but it was the best she could do.

After brushing her hair and applying the minimum of make-up up she sat down again at the window. The sun was sinking fast now; soon it would be dark. When Luciano entered after only the lightest tap on the door she shot up from her seat and looked at him crossly. 'I could have been naked.'

'I guessed you'd be ready and waiting,' he said easily, walking across the room towards her. He had changed into a grey shirt and grey moleskin trousers and looked devastating, but Celena still glared.

'I am ready, but—waiting? I hardly think so. I cannot believe that I let you talk me into this.'

His mouth tightened. 'The family are anxious to meet you. I'd like it if you snapped out of that mood.'

'I feel pressured,' she said defensively.

He took her by the shoulders and she thought he was going to shake her; instead he said with surprising softness, 'There is no need.'

A shudder ran through her at his touch. Despite her fears she could not ignore the sensations he evoked; they thrilled unbounded through her body.

'You're trembling,' he said, and sounded surprised. 'Are you really so afraid?'

Celena grasped the excuse. 'Of course I am,' she whispered shakily. 'I'm terrified.'

'There is nothing to be frightened of,' he assured her. 'My family are very normal people, just like you and me.'

Normal! He was a Sicilian aristocrat; how could that be normal? 'I'll be on show,' she declared. 'They'll be watching, they'll be judging, they'll be—'

'They'll adore you,' he told her firmly.

She shook her head. 'You're the eldest; you've kept them waiting; I shall have a lot to live up to. They will expect someone special after all these years.'

'You are special,' he told her.

'But not special in the way they'll be thinking,' she insisted. Only special because he had selected her for the part! she thought.

'You're being ridiculous,' he grated, impatient now.

'I will be at your side; you need never feel that you are on your own.'

Of course he would be at her side—he would be watching her like a hawk, making sure that she did not let him down. She pushed him away from her and her eyes shot sparks of fire. 'If it gets too much and I fail, then don't blame me.'

'You will not let me down, Celena.' He was as imperious as his great-grandmother at that moment, and it was easy to see from where he had got his strength and the supreme confidence that whatever he wanted he could have.

The meal was every bit as bad as Celena had expected. Giacoma did not put in an appearance, but Filippo and Paolo, Luc's brothers, and Gabriella, his sister, all swamped her with questions. Their respective spouses were present too and all eyes were on her. Celena felt as though she was being put through a third degree.

'How did you meet Luciano?' asked Gabriella.

'How long have you known each other?' questioned Filippo.

'How soon do you plan to get married?' enquired Paolo.

'Do you work?'

'Do you have brothers and sisters?'

'What do your parents think of Luciano?'

And so it went on and on until Celena's head was in a whirl and she could neither eat nor drink nor answer any more questions.

Luciano put up his hand. 'I think that's enough,' he said in his most authoritative voice. 'There'll be plenty of time to talk to Celena.'

'Of course,' said Gabriella sympathetically. 'We must be confusing you. It's just that we've waiting so long for Luciano to announce his intention of getting married.

We can see now why he took his time. You're very beautiful, Celena. Your engagement party is going to be *the* biggest social occasion of the year. Simply everyone is coming.'

Celena's heart slammed against her ribcage and she looked swiftly and accusingly at Luciano. What engagement party? her eyes flashed. 'I think we ought to talk,' she grated under her breath.

'Later,' he muttered.

'*Now!*' she insisted.

He turned to his family and smiled. 'I'm afraid Celena has developed a headache. Will you excuse us?'

He took her outside into a walled courtyard that was lit by coach lamps set into the walls. She turned on him viciously. 'Something else you conveniently *forgot* to tell me?'

He shrugged, spreading his hands in a typical Latin gesture. 'It's nothing.'

'We're getting engaged and you say it's nothing,' she accused him furiously. 'You strung me along, knowing I wouldn't agree. God, I hate you. How could you do this to me? When would you have told me about *our* engagement? An hour beforehand?' She shook her head in anger and bewilderment. 'I can't take it in; it's unbelievable.' And as another, even darker thought struck her she said, 'Don't tell me you've fixed a date for the wedding as well?'

He shook his head emphatically. 'I wouldn't do that, Celena.'

'Wouldn't you?' Her eyebrows rose in furious disdain. 'I wouldn't put *anything* past you. My goodness, is it really so important?'

'To me it is,' he answered.

'Because you love your great-grandmamma.'

'That is right.'

She admired him for it but even so... Her blood

boiled. 'So much that you'd lie, that you'd pluck a strange girl off the street and *pretend* she is the love of your life?' Again she shook her head. 'I can't believe any of this. It's like a nightmare; I hope it is one. I hope I'm going to wake up and find myself back home, back in my old job, never having heard the name Luciano Segurini.' She turned away, walking over the old flagstones which had been worn smooth by countless footsteps before hers. She kicked at a loose pebble. 'I hate you, Luciano.'

'I didn't pluck you off the streets, Celena,' he said, and there was an edge of anger to his voice too. 'I chose you deliberately.'

'Because I resemble Simone?' she grated, not even looking at him.

He gave an exasperated sigh. 'It was one of the reasons.'

She glanced at him then, scornfully. 'When did you first see me and realise that I looked like your ex-lover?'

'At an advertising convention in Birmingham.'

Her fine brows shot up. 'That was over six months ago. You were going out with Simone then.'

'I know.'

But it hadn't stopped him looking at other girls! 'And so, when your relationship with Simone ended, you immediately thought of me—is that what you're saying?' she asked crisply. It sounded like a whole pack of lies.

Luciano nodded.

'I must have made quite an impression,' she returned drily.

'It wasn't the only time I saw you—or heard of you,' he confessed. 'Clayton Smythe is a personal friend of mine.'

Her boss at Hillier and Jones! She looked at Luciano

now in surprise. 'He never said, not even when I put in my notice. Was he aware of your plans?'

'Only that I wanted you to work for me,' he told her.

Thank goodness for that, she thought. It was bad enough being duped into all of this without someone else knowing about it before her.

'I think you're a swine,' she said furiously.

'But you won't let me down.' It was a statement of fact, a warning, and his eyes glittered dangerously. He was being very calm but all hell would break loose if she dared to refuse.

Celena's chin lifted. 'I'm in a dilemma, aren't I? You've cornered me. I either tell everyone what a bastard you are and hurt your precious great-grand-mamma or I go along with it. There is no other choice.' And the trouble was that she already liked Giacoma; she did not want to hurt this grand old lady. 'The point is, Luc, how long are you expecting me to keep up this pretence?'

'Only until after the engagement party,' he assured her.

Could she believe him? He had not once told her the whole story; first it had been just a job, then would she please pretend to be his girlfriend, now she was expected to agree to becoming his fiancée. And what next? He had denied the marriage bit but could it be what he had in mind? Would she do herself a great disservice if she carried on with this play-acting? Would she end up in his bed, bearing his children? The thought was too horrifying to contemplate.

'How can I trust you?' she asked, grey eyes still fierce. 'You've already forced me into coming here—maybe not physically, but with clever words and subtle persuasion.'

'Forced you, Celena?' he asked, black brows rising,

tone brusque. 'It was your decision—yours alone. Are you suggesting that you are easily led?'

She let her breath out in an angry hiss. 'I can't win with you, can I?'

'There are no winners and losers,' he said. 'All I'm asking is a favour. You'll be amply rewarded.'

'I don't want rewarding,' Celena snapped. 'I don't want anything. I just want to be left alone to get on with my life as I used to.'

'We cannot put the clock back.'

'More's the pity,' she riposted. 'I rue the day I ever set foot in your office.' She could, of course, walk out of here right now and leave him to face the consequences, but because she was human and sympathetic, and because it involved other people besides herself, she knew that she would not do it. She moved away from him, staring at the ground, deep in thought. She paced the whole perimeter of the courtyard—and ended up back at Luciano's side.

'Well?' he asked impatiently.

Celena heaved a sigh. The decision had been made for her. Two button-bright eyes and a pair of gentle, gnarled hands had done their persuasion. 'I'll carry on the pretence,' she said slowly.

The harsh angles of Luciano's face relaxed, and he took her hands in his. 'You won't regret this, Celena.'

'I already have,' she told him coolly, snatching herself away, ignoring the tingle that ran through her. 'I'm only doing it for your great-grandmother.'

'As am I,' he reminded her tersely.

They walked around the courtyard together, Celena admiring the delicate white blossoms of the quince, their petals resting gently on shiny green leaves, and the bright yellow lemons that she had never seen growing before, and, below them, the purple tips of lavender just coming into flower. It would have been a peaceful place had it not been for Luciano.

His presence deeply disturbed her. She was in a situation that was proving more and more difficult as time went by. What had begun as an exciting new job had ended in her promising to marry Luciano—at least in the eyes of his family!

Gabriella came out to find them. Like each of his siblings she had glossy dark hair and an olive skin, though her face was much plumper and rounder than her elder brother's and she was nowhere near as tall. In fact she was quite dumpy. Nevertheless she had a warm and friendly personality and she looked at Celena now anxiously.

'We are all worried about you, Celena. We talk so much; we feel it is our fault you have a headache. How are you feeling? Perhaps you ought to lie down. I will send Francesca with some pills.'

'Please,' said Celena at once, 'it's not your fault. We've done a lot of travelling today; it's probably that.'

'You must look after her, Luciano,' Gabriella admonished him.

'Indeed I intend to.' He put his arm about Celena's shoulders and pulled her to him. 'She is the most important person in my life.' With a tender smile he pressed a kiss to her brow—and there was nothing Celena could do about it.

'And so she should be,' retorted his sister. 'We have waited a long time for you to find yourself a wife. He is so choosy,' she said to Celena. 'We have found him many girls over the years, but no, he is waiting for the right one. And now you are her. We all approve; I think you should know. We are looking forward to your engagement party tomorrow.'

Tomorrow! Another bombshell! Celena tried to tear herself away from Luciano but his arm tightened and she had to wait until Gabriella returned to the house before she could break free.

'You didn't tell me the party was tomorrow,' she said accusingly. She was not even being given time to get used to the idea. 'How long has it been arranged?'

'About a month,' he replied with a shrug. 'Does it really matter?'

'Of course it matters,' she retorted. One month! Not long after she had accepted his job offer. Lord, what unique confidence the man had. And how could she have been so blind as not to suspect that something was going on? 'How many will be coming to the engagement party?' she asked coldly.

'I have no idea,' he answered. 'We have many cousins and aunts and uncles, nieces and nephews too, and then there are friends—people who have known me since childhood. Well over a hundred, I imagine.'

Celena groaned and closed her eyes. All of them watching her and talking about her! 'Have you any real idea how much you're asking of me?'

'I'll be at your side,' he reminded her tightly. 'I have every confidence in you.'

Which was no consolation as far as Celena was concerned. It would still be a difficult situation. How could she pretend a love she did not feel? He was her boss, for goodness' sake, not her lover. He was paying her to do it, and that's all it was—a job of work.

Maybe if she kept telling herself that, kept reminding herself that she wouldn't get paid unless she did it properly then it would help her to get through the next couple of days.

'I'd like to go back to my room,' she said softly now. She felt exhausted and could think of nothing nicer than lying down between cool, sweet-smelling sheets.

'I'll show you the way,' he said at once.

'You needn't bother.'

'And you must say goodnight to the others.'

Celena groaned inwardly at the thought of facing his family again, but she dutifully popped her head round the door, receiving nothing but sympathy and good wishes, making her feel a small degree better.

'And now Bisnonna,' he said.

Was there no end to it? thought Celena unhappily.

Giacoma was ready for bed, dressed in a long, voluminous cotton nightdress, with a crocheted shawl around her shoulders. '*Buona notte*, my child. Sleep well, and tomorrow we will have a long talk. I will give you my congratulations in private as I shall put in only a brief appearance at your party; it is all too much for me these days.'

'I think you're wonderful,' said Celena impulsively as she kissed the old lady's papery cheek.

Giacoma looked pleased, Luciano looked pleased, and when they had left he said to Celena, 'You said exactly the right thing. Thank you.'

'I wasn't acting,' she retorted swiftly. 'I meant it. I like her.'

'And she seems to have taken a fancy to you.' He seemed well satisfied with the way things were turning out.

They reached her room. 'Goodnight,' Celena said stiffly.

'Is that a dismissal?' he asked with a faint frown.

'Very much so,' she told him. Surely he didn't expect her to invite him in?

'Don't I get so much as a goodnight kiss?' Thick brows rose questioningly. 'We are about to be betrothed, after all.'

Celena glared. 'I only play the game when someone's watching.'

Surprisingly his lips twitched. 'I think you should practise in case you slip up.'

'And I think you're taking a liberty,' she declared fiercely, yet at the same time the thought of Luciano's lips on hers sent a quiver of excitement through each and every one of her limbs.

'You have a beautiful mouth.'

Her heart quickened its beat.

'It's simply begging to be kissed.'

Panic set in. 'I'm tired; I want to—'

'But surely not too tired for this?' Luciano's eyes darkened as he cupped her face with warm, long fingers and bowed his head towards hers.

CHAPTER FOUR

CELENA stood transfixed as Luc's mouth inched closer; her breathing deepened and her body waited, and although she knew that it was a mistake, knew that she ought to resist him, that she ought to have shot inside her room and closed the door the moment he made his intentions clear she made no move.

Could he hear the pounding of her heart? she wondered. Was she giving away her inner turmoil? Was she letting him see how easily he aroused her?

The touching of his lips to hers was sweet, sweet torture, his kiss more poignant than any other. She closed her eyes and tried to will herself not to respond, but the kiss lasted for longer than she'd expected— gentle yet agonising, the lightest touch yet as searing as a branding-iron. He was subtly and stealthily taking possession of her, making sure that she did not let him down in front of his family.

She made a sound of protest in the back of her throat but he did not lift his head. She pushed her hands against the solid wall of his chest but he did not move. Instead his hands slid behind her so that she was imprisoned in the circle of his arms—and all the time his mouth continued to assault hers.

Downstairs Celena could hear voices as the family party broke up. They each had their own apartments in this huge old house and Luciano had assured her that it worked very well, that it was big enough to accommodate them all without their paths often crossing.

How it happened Celena did not know, but somehow she found herself inside her room with the door firmly closed. She was pinned against the wall and Luciano's kisses became more urgent.

In vain she renewed her struggles. This was insanity; she ought never to have allowed the kiss in the first place. She managed to free her mouth. 'Luciano, stop! Let me go! You cannot do this.'

'Oh, but I can,' he said with a confident smile. 'I am finding the whole experience decidedly pleasurable.'

'Well, I am not,' she declared stoutly, 'and I demand that you—'

Her sentence was cut short as his mouth claimed hers once more. It was a drugging kiss, reaching right down to the pit of her stomach, creating sensations that threatened to run out of control. She had to do something.

With all the strength she could muster Celena again pushed against him. 'You swine, let me go,' she hissed through gritted teeth.

'It's a pity you're not enjoying it too,' he said. 'It could make a difference to everything.'

'I enjoy your kisses like I'd enjoy those of a rattle-snake,' she flared. 'You have no right to do this to me. It's not part of the agreement at all.'

'How can we become successfully engaged if you fight me?' he asked softly, but as always there was steel beneath the velvet; he was not pleased by her reaction.

'What we do in front of your family is very different from what happens in private,' she declared strongly. 'Get out of here now or I shall refuse to take any further part in your game.'

He thrust her from him savagely, his jaw tight, eyes hard. 'Don't threaten me, Celena,' he rasped. 'You're in too deep now to back out.'

'Then don't force yourself on me,' she spat. 'You're going entirely the wrong way about getting me on your side.'

His eyes narrowed. 'Perhaps you'd like to tell me what I should do.' His voice was loaded with sarcasm.

'Leave me alone,' she retorted, 'except when it is strictly necessary.'

'But that would mean an awkwardness between us,' he countered harshly. 'I want us to feel right together; I want you to enjoy the feel of my body against yours; I want it to look natural, and I—'

Celena interrupted him fiercely. 'You think that by forcing your kisses on me now I'll—?'

'I wasn't aware that I was using force,' he cut in peremptorily. 'You're fighting yourself, Celena. I know that you're not completely immune to me. I know that if you relaxed you could enjoy my kisses. That is all I am asking—nothing more.'

For the time being, she thought bitterly. These things had a habit of snowballing. One kiss led to another; several kisses could lead to making love. It would be all too easy to give way when her body reacted as it did. She had to be strong; for her own sake she had to keep her feelings well hidden.

'I won't let you down,' she insisted.

His mouth tightened. 'Just see that you don't,' he warned darkly, and left the room.

Celena did not care that she had angered him. It was very important that she make her point. She did not want him to kiss her whenever and wherever he felt like it. She did not agree that it was a necessary part of his plan. He was taking advantage; he was a man with a healthy male appetite, and although he excited her to a very high degree no good could come out of submitting to his kisses.

The room felt empty when he had gone, though quite how he had managed to fill it with his presence in just those few short minutes she did not know.

She undressed and took another shower, scrubbing

mercilessly at her skin, needing to wash the feel of Luciano from her. It was impossible. She even fancied that she could still smell his aftershave. How was she going to sleep feeling like this?

For over half an hour she stood at the window in her nightdress looking out across the Sicilian countryside. Here and there was a pinpoint of light, but in the main it was dark and secret and mysterious.

This room probably held many secrets, but were any as strange as this arrangement she had with Luc? It was certainly something she would remember for the rest of her life—but whether the memories would be happy or distressing had yet to be discovered.

Eventually she crawled into bed, but sleep did not come easily; thoughts of tomorrow and the party that had been arranged troubled her deeply. Agreeing to be Luc's girlfriend had been one thing, but going through the performance of an official engagement was something else. It went completely against her nature to take part in such a total deception.

There was only she and Luc at the breakfast table the next morning. Francesca had woken her earlier with a tray of tea and Celena had joined Luc as soon as she was washed and dressed.

'Bisnonna always takes breakfast in her apartment,' he told her, when she questioned the fact that they were alone. 'In fact she rarely leaves it these days. She has requested you go and see her after we've eaten. You really made a big hit with her yesterday.' He looked pleased.

'Do we have to go through with this ridiculous engagement?' Celena asked hopefully as she helped herself to a croissant, discovering to her surprise that it was already filled with jam.

Dark eyes narrowed. 'But of course; it is why we are here,' he answered crisply.

'I shall never forgive you for tricking me,' she slammed out.

His jaw tightened. 'You're beginning to bore me, Celena. It was necessary.'

Because she wouldn't have agreed otherwise! 'And what am I going to wear?' she lamented. 'I never expected to take part in such a—a farce.'

'We'll go shopping,' he announced, his tone brusque. 'At the same time it will be my pleasure to show you some of our beautiful island.'

'It won't be mine,' she muttered beneath her breath. None of this was a pleasure.

His brown eyes watched her and he frowned harshly. 'Are you tired? Did you not sleep well?'

She flashed him an impatient glance. 'What do you think? I hardly slept at all, worrying about tonight.'

'My beautiful Celena, there is nothing to worry about.' His voice was softly persuasive now. 'Everyone will be besotted with you; all you have to do is relax and enjoy yourself—by my side, of course. Never forget that you are supposed to be in love with me.'

And he was supposed to be in love with her! What a joke! 'I'll hang onto your arm and gaze into your eyes all evening,' she told him glibly.

His face hardened. 'This is serious, Celena. I don't want you *over*doing it.'

'Perhaps you should have employed a professional actress.'

'Don't be ridiculous,' he snarled.

Celena's fine brows rose. 'It's no more ridiculous than *me* pretending to be in love with you.' She took a bite of her croissant and wiped her mouth on a napkin.

'I hoped—I really hoped,' he said, his face taut with anger, 'that by now you would have begun to feel at ease with me, that you would have learned to like me a little, that feigning love for me would come easy.'

'Maybe if you'd been straight with me from the beginning I might have done,' Celena retorted acidly. 'As things stand, I've had no time to get used to the idea of becoming your *fiancée*.'

A muscle jerked in his jaw. 'I thought it was best this way.'

'You thought wrong.'

'Obviously. At least we have the whole day in front of us.' And in sudden warning he added, 'Don't think about letting me down, Celena.'

It was on the tip of her tongue to ask what he would do if she did, but what point was there in antagonising him further? She remained silent, finishing her roll and sipping her coffee, and when breakfast was over she dutifully went up to see Giacoma.

The old lady motioned Celena to sit on a chair in front of her. 'I have done nothing but think about you all night,' she said. 'You're such a pretty girl, Celena, but it is to be expected. My Luciano, he likes beautiful things.'

Celena smiled weakly.

'I am happy for him now. He worried me. I thought his work meant more to him than a wife and a family. In Sicily our families are very important to us. I cried many tears for my Luciano. But now I can see that he has chosen well. Make him happy, my child; he is very precious to all of us.'

'I will,' she whispered. What else could she say under the circumstances? But she hated the lie. She felt dreadful hearing Luc's great-grandmother pour out her heart.

'Luciano has kept us waiting for too many years,' the woman went on. 'He should have many *bambini* by now. I will die a happy woman when he produces a son.'

Alarm rose inside Celena, closing her throat, panicking her heart. Goodness, the woman had already got them married.

Giacoma Segurini took Celena's hand, oblivious to the numbing effect of her words. Her fingers were icy-cold and felt brittle, as though they would snap at the merest pressure. 'Tell me about your own family,' she said, and was genuinely sorry when she heard that apart from her sister Celena had no one.

'There are many of us,' she said with a smile. 'We will be your family. You are very welcome; I am beginning to love you already.'

Celena felt herself warming to this woman also, despite her talk about babies, and she could see why Luciano loved and respected her. When their expected marriage never took place she would feel awful.

Later, in the close confines of Luciano's Mercedes, Celena found it difficult to ignore his overt sexuality. Despite everything, he had got beneath her skin. He was like a drug and she swallowed him in and her whole body became uplifted. Nevertheless she made her voice resentful. 'Your great-grandmother seems to be under the impression that we're going to get married and have babies without delay.'

To her astonishment he laughed. 'My *bisnonna* says these things; you must take no notice.'

'She was very serious,' replied Celena indignantly.

'I've no doubt she was,' he agreed. 'It's her dearest wish.'

'So what are you going to do about it?'

'No one can force us into marriage, Celena,' he said, still sounding amused.

'I'm glad to hear it,' she announced, but her thoughts were troubled. What if the family pressure became too great? What if he did ask her to go through with it? She wouldn't not even if he got down on bended knee, not even if he offered her a million pounds. She would not sell her body for anyone, even if it meant Davina leaving her school, even if it meant disappointing Giacoma. She was silent for the rest of the journey.

In Catania, Sicily's second largest city, Luciano seemed to know exactly where to find the best dress shop, and in no time at all he had the assistants dancing attendance.

He insisted that Celena parade in front of him wearing in turn each of the several different dresses that he had chosen from a selection brought to them.

Most were figure-flattering and highly decorative, and she liked none of them, but in the end he chose a simple black dress with narrow shoulder straps. It hugged the curves of her body to mid-thigh, before swirling out in a fantail almost to her ankles at the back but remaining knee-high at the front. The skirt section was lined in silver taffeta and rustled as she walked. A pair of black satin high-heeled shoes completed the ensemble.

It would not have been her own choice but Celena had to admit that it looked good. Nothing carried a price tag but she knew that it would be horrendously expensive. It was that type of shop.

'Is there anything else that you need?' he asked.

She shook her head.

'How about your hair? I know how much importance you women attach to such things.'

'I can do it myself,' she said.

'There is an excellent hairdresser here in—'

'I can manage,' she insisted.

'Make-up? Lingerie? Anything at all?'

'No.'

He seemed surprised. 'Not many girls are like you, Celena.'

She shrugged. 'I can't let you waste your money. You've already spent enough that wasn't necessary.'

'Not necessary?' A mocking brow rose. 'Everyone will be dressed up tonight. As my sister so rightly pointed out, it is *the* most important date in their calendar.'

'And it's all phoney,' she pointed out.

'But no one knows that,' he reminded her sharply. 'You'll be the most beautiful girl present; I shall be proud of you, and I'm honoured that you've agreed to do this thing for me. My *bisnonna* is happy too. She is delighted with my choice. You've certainly made a big hit with her.'

Celena smiled weakly.

'Now, let us explore the city,' he said with an abrupt change of subject. 'I don't think there'll be time to do Mount Etna as well, but another day, perhaps.'

Perhaps not, thought Celena. Another day— tomorrow, with a bit of luck—she would be home.

Catania was very sombre and grey, with both the buildings and paving-stones made from the lava that had spewed from Mount Etna. They looked around the cathedral and viewed the fine buildings of the university, and from Via Elnea, Catania's main street, Luciano pointed out the great cone of Etna in the distance. They wandered around the castle and its museum, they had lunch in a busy restaurant, and finally he declared that it was time to go home.

'I want you to rest. I don't want you to be too tired to enjoy our party this evening.'

Celena said nothing. She would not enjoy it under any circumstances. She did not want to attend the party, full stop. It promised to be the biggest ordeal of her life.

All the way back to his family home she remained silent, ignoring Luciano's attempts to make conversation, and the closer they got to Enna, the more miserable she became. The town was built on a narrow plateau running along the crest of the mountain and the road rose and fell like a switchback up towards it, running through woods which were carpeted with ferns and a scattering of rosemary bushes.

Once at the villa she scrambled out of the car with unnecessary haste, not even heeding Luciano's sharp, 'Celena!' as she hurried into the house. She wanted to be free of him for a few hours; she needed time to herself, to gather her tormented thoughts, to compose herself for the evening that lay ahead.

But she did not escape. He followed her to her room, closing the door behind him as he stepped inside. 'Celena, pull yourself together,' he commanded.

Her eyes sparked as she looked at him. 'How can I, under the circumstances?'

'You're making things very difficult for me.'

'And you think it isn't difficult for me?' she flashed.

He spread his hands. 'All I'm asking is a few hours of your time, a few hours' pretence. Is that too much for you?'

She eyed him coolly. 'Who's to say there won't be more?'

He frowned harshly. 'Is that what is troubling you?'

'The whole thing is,' she flung furiously.

'I thought you'd have got used to the idea by now.'

'Well, I haven't, and I won't—not ever. You went about it the wrong way and I can't do it.'

His face hardened, became even more angular, his dark eyes glittering abrasively. 'You cannot back out now. I forbid it.'

'You *forbid* it?' asked Celena incredulously. 'If I walk

out of here right now there is not a thing you can do about it.'

Thick brows rose. 'Is that what you think?' There was warning savagery in his eyes. 'I have gone to a lot of trouble to see that my *bisnonna* is made happy; I will not have you ruining things at this last hour.'

Celena felt a quiver of fear run through her. 'What are you saying?'

'That if necessary I will detain you here by force,' he told her grimly. 'I will not be made a fool of; I will not upset Bisnonna; you *will* pretend to be my fiancée whether you like it or not. Is that clear?'

Celena met Luciano's eyes defiantly. 'Maybe you can hold me here, but you cannot force me to co-operate.'

'But you will,' he warned.

She lifted her narrow shoulders. 'I think I might quite enjoy seeing you suffer.'

'It wouldn't only be me,' he growled. 'It would be my precious *bisnonna* too, and I will not have that, at any cost.'

And in truth Celena did not want to hurt the old woman either, but couldn't he understand the enormity of the undertaking? Maybe she could have handled a small, private, family party, but over a hundred people—all wanting to meet her, all intensely curious. How could she put on an act under such circumstances? How could she pretend to love Luciano when she was being so closely watched?

'Celena.' His voice changed, became soft all of a sudden, and gently persuasive. 'For Giacoma's sake if not mine.'

She closed her eyes, desperately wanting to shut him out, then the next second she gave a start of surprise when his palms cupped her cheeks. Her heart skittered along at twice its normal rate, not simply because she was afraid but because his touch was evoking that violent chemical reaction which was her downfall. Fear and excitement trembled through her limbs and when his head bowed down, when his lips claimed hers she knew that she could put up no further argument.

The kiss lasted an age, unsettling her body and eliciting a response that she would rather not have made. She became helpless as his arms slid around her, as the kiss deepened, as her lips parted and her body urged itself towards him.

'That's better,' he muttered gruffly. 'Much better. Keep this up, Celena, and we'll have no problem.'

'You're a swine,' she hissed fiercely, wanting to reject him but unable to find the strength to do so.

'And you're a surprisingly sensual young woman. Having you respond to me like this is a totally unexpected bonus.' His teeth gleamed as he smiled in triumph. 'Now that I have discovered your secret maybe you won't find it so hard pretending to be my fiancée after all.'

She shook her head in violent protest. 'If you think I will let you molest me in front of your family you're dreadfully mistaken.'

His eyes glinted angrily. 'I think they would appreciate us—kissing.'

'And I think you're a bas—'

His mouth on hers effectively shut her up, and just as effectively set her senses clamouring once again. Knowing now that he had the power to arouse her, Luciano took advantage, his hands sliding a warm caress over her back, his lips persuasive, exerting his influence as only a man confident of his own sexuality could.

Celena felt herself responding against her will, felt the full impact of him, felt her body reaching almost a fever pitch of emotion. And when a hand slid tormentingly over her breast, when a thumb teased and tortured her already erect and aching nipple she felt a moan escape the back of her throat and her hips surged against his.

'My beautiful, beautiful Celena,' he muttered, and he began to slide down the straps of her suntop, his mouth beating an agonising trail down the column of her throat.

His intentions were all too clear, and enough was enough, decided Celena. She had to stop him before things got out of hand, before she allowed intimacies she would later regret.

She had never before indulged her body in such a way, never felt a chemical reaction such as this—and to be used for the purpose of humouring Luciano's great-grandmother, as well as convincing his endless friends and relations that he had at last found the woman he wanted to marry, went very much against the grain. Pretence was one thing, actually playing out the part in full biological detail was another.

'Get away from me, Luc,' she gritted fiercely. 'What game do you think you're playing?'

'I'm helping you,' he said with a cynical smile.

'This sort of help I can do without,' she spat.

'I need to make sure you won't ruin things this evening.'

'Carry on like this and I'll do more than ruin it,' she warned.

Luciano grinned. 'Don't you like me knowing what a sexual little kitten you are?'

Her eyes flashed. 'You're despicable.'

And just as suddenly his smile faded. 'Be ready for eight, Celena. And don't forget—you're the star of the show.' He left the room abruptly and Celena collapsed on to the bed. She felt mortally humiliated. How could she have been so transparent? Why had she let him see how much he affected her? What had she done?

Without a doubt he would shamelessly play on her weakness; he would use it to his advantage at every opportunity. There was no way out of the situation.

She lay back and closed her eyes but Luciano was as clear in her mind as if he were still in the room. The impact he had made in so short a space of time was such that it would be with her for the rest of her life. She doubted if any man she met in the future would have such an instant and devastating effect on her senses.

Later Francesca brought her a tray of tea and home-baked macaroons which were delicious, and finally Celena took a shower and washed her hair. She debated whether to wear it in her usual style, hanging loose about her shoulders, or to sweep it up. She tried on the dress and in the end decided that it would look better piled on top of her head.

At five minutes to eight, when Luciano tapped on her door, she was ready. A last look in the mirror had revealed a tall, sophisticated stranger, with enormous grey eyes, lids brushed with grey shadow to emphasise their beauty, deep pink lipstick and blusher and a pair of gold hoop earrings completing the ensemble.

None of her apprehension showed; she looked calm and controlled—a different person in fact. The expensive dress, unlike any she had ever worn before, had given her confidence, and she stood tall as she faced Luciano in the doorway.

He silently appraised her, taking in every detail, missing nothing, causing a riot of sensation inside her, which still, somehow, even though it happened every time, managed to take her by surprise. Her limbs felt as though they were turning to jelly and she was glad when he spoke.

'You're every man's dream, Celena. I am proud of you.'

Although his words meant nothing personal, although they were simply thanks because she was carrying out the part he had picked for her, she could not help feeling a glow of pleasure. She smiled weakly. 'Thank you.'

Luciano looked good himself in dark trousers and a white dinner jacket—lethally attractive, doing things to her that should never be allowed. She found it difficult to take her eyes off him.

He closed the door and moved towards her and Celena felt something approaching panic stir her heart. Please God he wasn't going to kiss her again. It wasn't necessary—she was already aroused, already prepared to play to the full the part of his fiancée.

She had thought of nothing but him during the last few hours, had relived his kisses and the torture of his hands. She was so aware of him that it was unbelievable, her whole body pulsing and tingling, as if the lightest touch would ignite her.

'I'd like you to wear these,' he said, producing a well-worn leather box in which nestled a pair of diamond drop earrings and a matching necklace. 'They belong to Bisnonna; she wants you to have them.'

They were exquisite and obviously worth a small fortune. Celena gasped and shook her head. 'I can't; it wouldn't be right.'

'You will upset her if you refuse.'

'But—' she felt breathless at the sheer beauty of them '—under the circumstances, I couldn't—'

'No one knows the circumstances,' he cut in tightly, a warning flash in his eyes.

'What if I lost them? What if—?'

Again he interrupted. 'What if nothing,' he rasped.

'You say Giacoma wants me to have them—to *keep* them?'

He inclined his head. 'An engagement present.'

'But I couldn't do that,' she squeaked.

His eyes narrowed on hers. 'It's all part of the pretence.'

Celena held his gaze and then pulled a wry face. 'Of course.' He would take them back just as soon as the whole charade was over. Slowly she removed her gold hoops and held out her hand for the diamond earrings. To her consternation Luciano insisted on fixing them himself.

The brush of his fingers against her throat and ears sent desire coursing through her bloodstream, and when he stood behind her to fasten the heavy antique necklace, the aching pleasure of his touch was almost more than she could bear.

When he had finished she moved away quickly, saw his faint smile, and knew that he had guessed the reason for her withdrawal. She took a further, final look at herself in the full-length mirror, and this time, as well as seeing a beautiful stranger, she saw a woman whose cheeks were flushed, whose eyes radiated desire, and she felt appalled at her own transparency.

Did Luciano manage to arouse all women just by a touch? Or was she different? Was there something in her make-up that reacted to him like liquid mercury to variations in temperature? It helped, undoubtedly, in the part she had to play, but it could prove embarrassing in time.

'Let us go,' he said, and on the landing Celena heard the sonorous sound of a clock striking eight.

He took her arm as they descended the ornate staircase and led her towards two huge swing-doors which had previously remained closed. Quite what she was expecting Celena did not know, but certainly not this huge ballroom filled to overflowing with people all looking expectantly in their direction.

CHAPTER FIVE

IT WAS as though someone had announced them and if Luciano had not been holding her Celena would have turned tail and fled. She had expected it to be an ordeal but this was even worse. She had hoped that they would slip into the party unobtrusively, that they would mingle and be introduced casually; she had never for one moment expected this grand entrance.

They were poised at the top of another flight of steps and for a moment there was silence, complete and utter silence, every eye on her. Then came the unexpected sighs of approval, exclamations of pleasure, delight at the beautiful girl whom Luciano had chosen for himself.

He looked at her, pleased, and there on the steps he kissed her. Their guests applauded. Luciano held up his hand and in the ensuing silence he introduced Celena to them.

She wished the floor would open and swallow her up, she wished he had prepared her, and when, with a flourish, he plucked a small leather box out of his pocket, snapping it open to retrieve an antique diamond ring that perfectly matched the necklace and earrings, Celena felt even more uncomfortable.

A breathless hush filled the room as he took her hand and slid the ring onto it, and then there was a wild, joyous cheer. Champagne appeared, sparkling in delicate crystal glasses with the Segurini crest engraved on them, and Giacoma—a proud Giacoma who had appeared suddenly at their side—announced the toast. 'To my precious Luciano, and his beautiful Celena. I wish you both happiness.'

'Happiness,' endorsed every person in the room.

Luciano led her onto the floor so that they could begin the dancing. He was expert and Celena found it easy to follow him. It was as though there were wings on her ankles; she felt as light as thistledown and if she closed her eyes she could almost forget the sea of faces watching them.

'You're enchanting,' he whispered in her ear, but Celena knew that it was all part of the game, and when, one by one, his various friends and relatives came up to them to be introduced she thought the evening was never going to end.

Her face ached with the effort of keeping a permanent smile on her lips, it was confusing trying to remember names, but the hardest thing of all was pretending to be deeply in love with Luciano.

If he hadn't remained at her side, if he hadn't answered questions she found too difficult, if he hadn't constantly smiled at her and held her and brushed kisses on her cheek, she would have failed, undoubtedly. He kept the fires alight inside her by his tenderness and thoughtfulness, and in the circle of his arms it was easy to pretend. Halfway through the evening he suggested they take a walk in the garden.

When they were finally alone his hand dropped from her elbow, telling Celena all too clearly that his attentiveness indoors was all an act. She felt suddenly bereft. She had hoped, a little, that what had started off as pretence would result in his feeling a faint attraction to her too. It was obviously not the case.

He took a few steps away, leaning back against a balustrade on the edge of the terrace, surveying her calmly. 'You're doing well, Celena.'

'I'm only doing what I'm getting paid for,' she retorted sharply.

An eyebrow rose. 'Was I wrong in sensing that you were actually *enjoying* yourself?'

'Totally,' Celena assured him. 'How can I enjoy being paraded like a clown in a circus? I feel like a curiosity. I sincerely hope I never meet any of them again afterwards; the embarrassment would be too much to handle.'

Her harsh words angered him; a muscle jerked fiercely in his jaw, his dark eyes glittering through narrowed lids. 'I can assure you that no one regards you as anything abnormal. In fact I have heard nothing but praise. I've been congratulated over and over again on finding such a beautiful girl. But, hell, who cares what they think so long as my *bisnonna* is happy?'

Giacoma had not stayed at the party long but her pleasure had been obvious. She had insisted Celena sit at her side, and she had told her time and time again how happy she was that Luciano had at last found himself a bride. 'I trust the wedding will be soon?' she queried.

'We've made no plans yet,' Celena answered nervously, and now she brought up the subject. 'Your *bisnonna* has mentioned marriage again.'

'And I've no doubt she will go on mentioning it,' Luciano responded with a smile.

'I don't find it funny,' she declared fiercely. 'When do we go back to England—tomorrow?' She couldn't wait.

'Are you forgetting we still have work to do?'

Celena eyed him suspiciously. 'Are you telling me that the car account wasn't just a ruse to get me out here?'

'Not at all,' he assured her strongly. 'It's genuine business.'

'Which just happened to coincide with your *other* arrangements,' she remarked scornfully. 'Lord, I hate you, Luciano Segurini. I wish I'd never met you.' She felt a burning need to get away, to be on her own for a few minutes.

As if in answer to her prayers, someone called to Luciano that he was wanted on the telephone. 'You'd better come back inside,' he told her, looking annoyed at the interruption.

She shook her head. 'I'll wait here; I need the air.'

Uncertainly he left her and Celena turned and made her way across a well-kept lawn to a stone gazebo that during the day had commanding views over the valley. It was still and peaceful and faintly she could hear the band playing, and she could see in her mind's eye the ladies in their jewel-coloured dresses being whisked around the floor by their attentive male escorts.

She pondered how her life had changed in the matter of a few short weeks. It was hard to imagine that she was pretending to be the fiancée of a rich Sicilian aristocrat, that she was being accepted by his family and fêted as though she were a queen.

When footsteps approached Celena gave an inward groan. The phone call had been fatefully short; it had given her no time at all to collect her thoughts and restore some sort of peace to her mind.

But it wasn't Luciano who joined her. In fact they weren't a man's steps at all. It was a dark-haired girl about her own age who looked vaguely familiar and yet Celena could not remember having seen her before. The lamps that studded the grounds gave off sufficient light for her to see the girl quite clearly.

'I'll make it quick,' said her intruder, 'before Luciano comes back.'

Celena frowned. Make what quick? She was obviously English and extremely attractive. Luciano hadn't said that anyone from England was coming out for the party. Was she a friend of the family? Maybe she even lived here in Enna.

'You're wasting your time if you think Luciano will actually marry you,' said the girl bluntly. 'He doesn't love you, he loves me—and I love him. I made a stupid mistake, but once I tell him he will understand. He will—'

'*Simone!*' exclaimed Celena, her mouth dropping open. It was no wonder that she had thought she recognised her; Simone could have been her sister. There were certain differences—Simone's cheekbones were higher, her chin slightly more pointed, her hair a much darker shade of auburn—but. . .

'Uncanny, isn't it, how alike we look?' asked the girl. 'I thought that myself when I first saw you. It gave me quite a start. It proves Luciano was still thinking about me when he took up with you. And if we exchanged clothes now and I walked back into the party no one would know any difference.'

Celena wasn't so sure. Superficially they looked the same, but Simone spoke differently, she acted differently, she *was* different. 'What are you doing here?' she asked with a frown. 'Does Luc know?'

Simone shook her head. 'Not yet, and I suppose I sort of gatecrashed. But he will—soon. I'm here to claim him back. It's obvious he's told you about me.'

'Yes,' admitted Celena.

'It's been only two months since we split up, and here he is engaged to you,' said Simone nastily. 'I called his office and when they told me he was out here I knew I had to come. I certainly didn't expect to find all this going on, however. I find it very hard to believe; we had talked about marriage ourselves. You know about his inheritance, of course?'

Celena frowned. 'Inheritance? What inheritance?'

'He didn't tell you?' Simone's lips twisted into a confident smile. 'No, of course he wouldn't. You might not have agreed to go through with it.'

'I don't know what you're talking about,' said Celena, still frowning.

'I suppose he told you that it was love at first sight, that he had never met a girl like you before, and what was the point in waiting?'

Celena did not like the aggression in Simone's voice, but she said nothing.

'When his great-grandmother dies he will inherit all of this.' Simone spread her hands to take in the whole estate. 'It has always gone to the eldest male heir, provided he is married, of course. Otherwise it goes down the line. And Luciano really wants it; it is his dream, his ambition.'

'Luciano is a wealthy man in his own right,' Celena declared strongly. 'He doesn't need this place. I think you're wrong.'

'It's the prestige he's after,' Simone insisted. 'He told me all about it. His family have been going for hundreds of years. To be the head, to live in this house is worth more than all the riches in the world. The Segurinis are one of the oldest and most respected families in Sicily.'

It was a convincing story, and if he was really this desperate it all made sense—the way he had chased her after Simone let him down, the fact that he was paying her so handsomely. He had been cunning too, leading her into the situation slow step by slow step. No wonder he had said that her being chemically attracted to him was an added bonus. It would make things so much easier when he finally told her of his wedding plans.

She had no doubt now that it was all arranged—in his own mind at least. What he hadn't counted on was Simone turning up again.

'I'm sorry if I've upset you,' said Simone snidely. 'But I think you'll find that when Luciano discovers I've come back to him you will get your marching orders. It need make no difference here. I'll just take your place and no one will know.'

Celena had had enough. She lifted her chin and stared at her adversary haughtily. 'I wouldn't be so sure about Luciano not loving me if I were you.'

The girl looked startled. 'What do you mean? He can't possibly—'

'Celena, where are you?' Luciano's voice sounded through the darkness.

'In the gazebo,' she called, welcoming the intrusion, wondering what his reaction to Simone's presence would be.

He came to an abrupt halt when he saw the two of them, his eyes darting from one to the other. Finally he looked at Simone with a harsh frown. 'What the devil are you doing here?'

'Darling.' The girl stepped forward, her arms uplifted ready to drape themselves around his neck, but Luciano stepped away.

'I asked a question,' he said icily.

Simone gave a wry smile. 'I came to apologise. I was a beast; I should never have given you up. I love you, Luciano—I always have, I always will. Will you forgive me?' Her voice trembled with emotion and there were actually tears in her eyes.

She was a good actress, thought Celena.

Luciano looked at her coldly, completely unmoved by her plea. 'What's happened to your new lover? Has he seen through you too?'

'Darling, what do you mean?' purred Simone.

Luciano shook his head impatiently and changed the subject. 'How did you get into my party?'

Simone lifted her delicate shoulders. 'It was easy, sweetheart. So many people were arriving that one more made no difference.'

'How long have you been in Sicily?'

'I arrived only today.'

'And tomorrow you're going back to England.' It was a statement rather than a question, but Simone shook her head.

'I've booked into a hotel in Enna. I shall probably stay for a week, maybe longer. You've told me so much about Sicily that I simply must explore. It's a lovely country, Luciano, what I've seen of it so far. I could live here quite easily.'

Luc snorted savagely. 'You and I are finished, Simone; there is no going back. If it's your plan to wheedle your way into my life again then you're wasting your time.'

Her eyes flashed dramatically. 'You're actually going to marry Celena? You're saying that it's over between us—for good?'

Luc looked at Celena and she held her breath as she waited for his answer. 'I think it is time you went back to your hotel, Simone,' he said coldly. 'I will order you a taxi.'

The girl's chin came up and she threw a vicious glance in Celena's direction. 'There is no need; I can look after myself. But you needn't think that this is the last you will see of me, Luciano. I have no intention of giving up without a fight.' She strode away, her back straight, her head high.

'I apologise for the intrusion,' he said stiffly, once Simone was out of earshot.

'She's a very determined lady,' Celena responded.

His lips were grimly clamped and he watched Simone until she disappeared, and then with a visible effort he banished her from his mind. 'I've bad news, I'm afraid.'

Celena's first thought was that something had happened to Giacoma, that perhaps the excitement had been too much for her. Her hand fluttered to her throat.

'I have to go back to England—straight away. A

problem no one else can handle. I'm flying out early
tomorrow.'

And he called that bad news! As far as Celena was
concerned it was good. 'I'll be ready,' she said. 'I—'

His lifted hand stopped her. 'You're not coming.
Bisnonna would be distraught if you left so soon. I
promised her a few days. She will love having you to
herself, and I'll be back in forty-eight hours, maybe less.
I don't think that's too much to ask under the
circumstances.'

Celena's chin lifted. 'You cannot do this to me; you
cannot make me stay against my will.'

His eyes looked coldly into hers but, undeterred,
Celena went on, 'I'm sure you could appease Giacoma;
you can do no wrong in her eyes. Tell her we'll be
coming back, tell her anything, but I'm not staying here
without you. As far as I'm concerned I've done what
you asked. I'm wearing your ring—' it felt heavy and
strange on her finger '—I've paraded as your fiancée—
and that is all I am going to do.' Her tone became
brittle and she turned away.

It was an unbelievable situation. He had lied to her
all along—it wasn't love for his great-grandmother that
had prompted his absurd proposal but greed for power.
It was on the tip of her tongue to declare that she knew
what he was up to, but something stopped her. Maybe
it was a growing fondness for Giacoma. The woman
would be distraught if she ever found out what Luc was
doing—even distraught was too mild a word; she would
be devastated. It would destroy her completely—more
completely than Luc not getting married at all.

Luciano caught her shoulders and spun her round to
face him. 'What's got into you, Celena?' he demanded
tersely.

'Nothing,' she retorted. 'I just don't like being told
what to do. All along you've tricked me. What I thought

was a remarkable job offer has turned into a farce and I no longer want to be a part of it. I want to go back to England; I want to be free of you. Simone's turned up, offering herself to you on a plate. Take her; you deserve each other. I've had enough.'

His fingers gripped her shoulders even more tightly, hurting, bruising. 'Forget Simone,' he rasped. 'In the eyes of my family you are my fiancée; you cannot back out now.'

Her eyes flashed in his direction. 'No?'

'It is important to me.'

'I know it is,' she cried. 'A lot more important than you let me believe.'

His grip relaxed fractionally. 'I'm glad you understand, Celena.'

'Oh, I understand all right,' she answered, 'but it doesn't mean that I'm going to stay.'

'If you don't,' he growled, a sudden threat in his voice, 'you can kiss goodbye to your job at Luse, and I shall make it my personal business to see that you don't get another.'

Celena gasped, shocked that he was prepared to go to such lengths. 'That's blackmail!' she exclaimed.

His eyes glittered. 'This whole thing is very important to me.'

If Simone hadn't turned up and told her the truth Celena would have thought that he was being adamant because of his love for Giacoma; she might even have admired him. Now all she felt was cold contempt. But she also felt sympathy for the old lady who did not know what a monster her great-grandson had turned into. Perhaps she ought to warn her even?

More importantly, though, if she was blacklisted, if she could not get another job, she would be letting her sister down. And that was something she could not do. She must never lose sight of the fact that this was why she had taken the job in the first place. Keeping Davina at boarding-school was her top priority.

Celena sighed heavily. 'It looks as though I have no choice.'

Luc smiled, the light of triumph in his eyes. 'I'm glad you've come to your senses.'

'Senses be damned,' she snapped. 'You've got me trapped.'

He took her hand. 'Let's get back to the party.'

Facing all of his relatives again, especially now that she knew the truth, was the last thing Celena wanted. How many others knew what he was up to? How many were whispering behind their backs? How many were pitying her?

But she knew that refusal would heap further wrath on her shoulders, so she allowed herself to be led back inside; she smiled and chatted and did everything that was expected of her, but it was a relief when people started to drift away.

In turn each one of them came to say goodbye, to kiss her cheek and make comments about how clever she was in capturing Luciano when everyone else had failed. If only they knew, she thought; if only they knew.

She had hoped to be able to go straight to her room, was unprepared when Luciano suggested they have one last drink together. 'I'm tired,' she protested. 'I really would like to go to bed.'

But he pulled her into the study that he had used yesterday. 'We won't be disturbed here,' he said. 'This was always my room when I lived here and somehow it's been kept that way since.'

The room had a roll-top desk, deep armchairs and book-filled shelves. The lamp he switched on sent deep shadows scurrying into the corners and yet the room had surprising warmth. She could see why he liked it.

She perched herself on the edge of the well-polished chesterfield and Luciano poured her a glass of sherry from a crystal decanter. Celena did not particularly like sherry but she said nothing, taking the glass and twisting the spiral stem between her fingers.

'I think tonight was an unqualified success,' he said as he sat down beside her, 'despite Simone's surprising intrusion.'

Celena instantly wished that she had chosen a chair. To her dismay the animal attraction was still there. Regardless of finding out that Luciano wasn't the caring person she had thought, her awareness of him physically had not diminished. Her heart was already running at top speed. She took a sip of sherry and slid into the corner of the sofa, crossing her legs primly, hoping he would not notice her agitation.

It was a mistake. Luciano edged up also and she was trapped. He plucked the glass from her nerveless fingers and set it down on a small side-table, and then, half turning towards her, he took her hands into his.

'Do you think everyone believed we were genuine?' she pondered, and was surprised to hear how husky her voice sounded.

'I see no reason why not.' He looked surprised by her question. 'What makes you ask such a thing?'

She shrugged. 'Guilt, I guess.'

He smiled widely. 'My dear Celena, you were magnificent. No one could have possibly guessed that you're not in love with me.' His eyes looked steadily into hers. 'I actually think that you're worrying for nothing.' His thumbs stroked the back of her hands, increasing her tension, sending spirals of sensation through her stomach. 'Bisnonna loves you, and you clearly like her. I think the two of you will get along splendidly.'

'She might ask awkward questions,' worried Celena.

'Then we'll go through it all now so that you cannot

possibly make any mistakes. I told her that you work
for me and that's how we met, that we've known each
other for nine months—which was when I first met
Simone.' He covered every possible eventuality, shoot-
ing questions at Celena afterwards until he was convinced that she would not let him down.

'What if she mentions wedding plans again?' she
asked.

His mouth twisted. 'A strong possibility, I'm afraid.
Maybe you should humour her.'

Celena's eyes flashed. 'And put myself into a situation I cannot get out of?' Play right into his hands! she
thought. 'No, thank you.'

'Would marriage to me be so awful?'

'I always thought marriages of convenience were
confined to the pages of fiction,' she said scornfully. 'I
didn't think people actually did that sort of thing. I
wouldn't, ever—not ever.'

She sensed the tension in him and was pleased that
he felt uneasy. It served him right. He shouldn't even
consider deceiving his great-grandmother.

He looked into the glowing light of her eyes. 'I didn't
realise what a firebrand you were.'

'Really?' she asked, her brows lifting. 'Didn't your
magic computer tell you? I thought it knew everything
about me.'

His lips flickered grimly, but the next second he had
himself under control and he gave a smile of appreciation. 'Machines, unfortunately, do not take human
emotions into account.'

'So you took a risk that I'd be the right sort of
person?'

'I used my own judgement,' he told her, 'though I
have to admit to a few surprises—this being one of
them.' And before Celena could anticipate his intention

Luciano had imprisoned her in his arms and his mouth unhesitatingly found hers.

She wanted to fight, she wanted to show indifference, she wanted to pull away and run up to her room, but it was impossible. Her body refused to obey the instructions her mind sent to it, lying there foolishly and submitting. It was devastatingly, treacherously weak where this man was concerned.

Already she was being consumed by burning hunger, pulses beating erratically, heart thudding. For some unknown reason it felt good in his arms; she felt as though she was being uplifted—a glorious, light-headed sensation that took over all sane reasoning.

Even when his lips left hers to explore the delicate contours of her face she made no protest, merely lying in his arms, her breathing unsteady, her lips parted, her eyes closed. It was heaven and hell at the same time. It was torturing her but making her feel deliciously, heart-stoppingly feminine.

'You're quite an incredible woman,' he muttered, pressing tiny, exciting kisses to the edges of her mouth.

She made a faint sound of protest.

'Yes, you are, Celena. Quite incredible.' He pulled down her lower lip and kissed the soft flesh inside, and Celena knew that he was using devious methods to get what he wanted—but still she couldn't stop him.

It was remarkable, this hold he had somehow managed to gain over her. She had played right into his hands by feeling an instant biological attraction, and it was so strong that she could do nothing about it. Whenever he touched her it took over.

His mouth moved to scorch a trail down the aching column of her throat, and still she was putty in his hands, her head back against the sofa, her whole body pliant. She unconsciously whimpered her pleasure as he pressed kisses to her shoulders, as he nudged aside the thin straps of her dress.

Celena was in a world where nothing mattered except the senses. This was pleasure of a sort she had never experienced before. She held Luc's head between her palms, feeling the strong shape of him, threading her fingers through the coarse blackness of his hair, not even demurring when he slid the top of her dress down.

All she felt was an aching need, and when his hands reverently cupped her naked breasts her cry of pleasure became more intense and she urged his mouth towards her nipples.

It was sweet, sweet pleasure. It was torment beyond description. Her head spun as though she were spiralling into space, her whole body alive—tingling and glowing, responding and needing.

'Oh, Luc.' She clasped his head firmly as his teeth nibbled, as his tongue rasped, as his hands moulded.

He looked up at her when she spoke, and Celena saw a similar hunger, his eyes glazed, mouth wet and moist. He lifted himself up to capture her mouth again, causing a torturous ache in the pit of her stomach. Her lips clung to his, returning kiss for kiss, unashamedly letting him see the true depth of her desire.

When he turned his attention back to her throbbing breasts her head fell back and she gave herself up to the delirious ecstasy of the moment. If this was pure animal hunger, she mused, what would it be like if they were in love? It was a mind-blowing thought.

The torture went on for ever, neither wanting to put a stop to such excitement. Celena knew she had to be thankful that he went no further, because she would not have had the will-power to stop him. It was Luc himself who finally called a halt, dragging himself reluctantly away from her. 'If I don't stop now,' he muttered thickly, 'I won't be responsible for my actions.'

His words broke the spell and Celena began to slide down off her cloud. She tugged her dress up over her swollen breasts and said thickly, 'I must have had more to drink than I thought.'

'You're not drunk, Celena,' he assured her. 'You're simply following the dictates of your body. You're the most sensual woman I've ever met, and—'

'And I should have known better,' she cut in abruptly. 'I'm playing right into your hands, aren't I?'

He smiled with satisfaction. 'As I was saying earlier, discovering this side of you is one hell of a surprise. I have no complaints.'

Her eyes flashed as she slid her straps into place. 'I think you're taking advantage.'

'I wouldn't do that,' he assured her.

She stood up and straightened her dress. 'No?' she asked sceptically.

'I would have stopped any time you asked.' He got to his feet too and stood unnecessarily close—close enough for her to feel the exciting warmth of him, to inhale his heady masculine scent.

'Then if I tell you now that I don't want you to touch me again will you oblige?' she asked coolly.

His lips twisted. 'That's rather a tall order. You're a temptress, Celena—a witch.' His voice dropped to a growl. 'I don't think you're aware of your powers.'

She took a step backwards. 'You're talking rubbish,' she snapped. 'And I've had enough; I'm going to bed.' Otherwise she would end up in his arms again, she felt sure.

'You haven't finished your drink.'

'I don't want it,' she told him brittly, and headed for the door.

His voice halted her. 'I expect I will be gone before

you get up. I want your promise that you won't let me down.'

And that was all it amounted to, what this last few minutes had been about. It was the last straw as far as Celena was concerned. Losing her job and forcing Davina to drop out of boarding-school seemed of no importance compared with the humiliation she faced here. She was going back home tomorrow, with Luc or without him.

Not even deigning to answer, Celena ran lightly up the stairs and into her bedroom, leaning back against the door, her eyes closed, her breathing ragged.

She was a fool, an incredible fool. How could she have given herself to Luc like that? How could she have let him see how easily he aroused her? And all for nothing! He had no feelings for her whatsoever. He was using her; he was interested only in becoming head of the Segurini family.

She let the beautiful dress slip down her body to the floor. Normally fastidious about putting her clothes away, she left it lying there. It was a distasteful reminder of the evening's events.

Turning on the shower, she stood for several minutes letting the heated jets of water rain down on her. She hated herself for allowing Luc to invade her privacy, and she was even more disgusted by her own unfettered response. She felt ashamed and degraded, and what must he be thinking? That she gave herself like this to any man? That was even worse.

She crawled abjectly into bed but sleep had never been so far away, and when she did finally drop off it was to dream of Luc making love to her, and she woke early, drenched in sweat and even more agitated than before.

Another shower refreshed and cooled her but it did nothing for her mind. Still determined to leave, she quickly packed her suitcase, but when she opened the dressing-table drawer it was to discover that the wallet containing her passport was missing. She stood for a moment, stunned, until realisation dawned. There was only one person who could have taken it.

CHAPTER SIX

Luc must have foreseen that she might want to run away, thought Celena as she raced downstairs, desperately hoping that he had not yet left.

Luck was with her. Luc sat alone at the breakfast table, looking up in surprise when she erupted like a whirlwind into the room. 'Good Lord, Celena, what's the matter?'

'Where's my passport?' she demanded fiercely, almost skidding to a halt in front of him.

Thick brows rose and there was an abrupt stillness to him. 'And why would you want that?'

'You had no right taking it,' she exploded. 'My credit cards were in that wallet too.' She held out her hand. 'Give them back to me, right now.'

'I don't think so, Celena.'

'Why not?'

'I'm protecting my interests.'

'You mean you knew I might try to leave before you were ready to let me go?'

He inclined his head. 'There was every possibility. You're a very volatile young lady, although I did think after last night that—'

'It was last night that convinced me I was doing the wrong thing,' she interrupted hotly. 'I will not be used, Luc.'

'Is that what you think I was doing?' he asked, a bitter twist to his lips.

Her eyes flashed. 'Absolutely.'

'You think I'm capable of such inhuman emotions?'

'To get what you want, yes,' she riposted.

An eyebrow rose and fell again. 'I love my *bisnonna*, I want her happiness before anything else—and I thought you felt the same about your sister. Are you suggesting that you'd force Davina to leave her school for the sake of spending a few days here? It's a very selfish attitude, Celena; I'm sure she wouldn't thank you for it.'

He was right, of course, but it didn't make things easier. 'Damn you!' she cried passionately.

'Does that mean you will stay?'

Her grey eyes, as dark as a thundercloud, locked into his. 'I don't have much choice, do I? But I find the way you're treating me deplorable, and if your great-grandmother senses there is something wrong then don't blame me. I told you I'm no actress, and the longer I stay here the harder it is becoming.'

A muscle jerked in his jaw, her answer clearly not pleasing him. 'Sit down, Celena.' He poured a glass of chilled orange juice and placed it in front of her. 'Francesca will be in shortly; you can tell her what you'd like for breakfast.' He had dismissed their conversation as though it were of no consequence.

'I'm not hungry,' she muttered.

'I'm sure she'll find something to tempt your taste buds.' His gaze dropped to her hand as she picked up the glass. 'Why aren't you wearing your ring?' he asked sharply.

In actual fact Celena had forgotten. She had placed it in the box with the necklace and earrings last night for safe-keeping and hadn't even thought about it this morning. She shrugged. 'The party's over.'

'But not our engagement,' he grated through closed teeth. 'Fetch it—*now*.'

But at that moment Francesca entered and Celena had a deliberately long debate with her. She saw Luc keep looking at his watch and knew that any minute now he would have to leave. It really wasn't in her nature to be rebellious but the situation was getting to her and she felt a perverse sort of delight in angering him.

Finally Francesca left and Luc barked, 'Your ring, Celena.'

'I'll put it on after breakfast,' she answered. 'What does it matter?'

'It matters a great deal,' he growled.

'You mean it's symbolic, telling all the world that I belong to you?' Her eyes were scornful on his. 'I belong to no man, Luciano. I'm doing you a favour—a very big favour—and you'd best remember it. If you push me too far I shall tell your great-grandmother exactly what you're up to.'

His nostrils flared as he looked at her long and hard, his eyes glittering between narrowed lids, and she knew that he was seeing all his hopes and plans crashing to the floor. 'I don't think you'd be that unwise, Celena, not if you know what's good for you.' He scraped back his chair and stood up. 'And now I have to go.'

'Perhaps you ought to take me with you,' she suggested sweetly. 'In that way I won't be able to jeopardise your carefully laid plans.'

His bony fingers gripped her shoulders from behind. 'You won't do that, Celena,' he threatened, his voice close to her ear. 'You are to spend your time working on ideas for the new advertisement.'

And then, just as suddenly, he let her go, lifting her chin instead, kissing her warmly and possessively, as though no heated words had been exchanged. 'Goodbye, my sweet. I'll be thinking of you.'

He was gone before she could utter a response, but not before a searing heat invaded her body. When Francesca returned with her toast she was sitting with her eyes closed, still feeling the torment of his touch.

Later she paid Luc's great-grandmother a visit and the woman was delighted to see her. 'Come and sit down, my child,' she welcomed her. 'It is a great pity Luciano has been called away; nevertheless, it will give us the opportunity to really get to know each other.'

Celena smiled faintly and twisted the heavy ring she had put on her finger. It was slightly loose and she was afraid of losing it, but she knew that not to wear it would cause raised eyebrows. She was doing it for the old woman's sake, she told herself, not Luciano's.

'You were beautiful last night, my child—radiant. I was watching everyone as you entered the room. What an impression you made. Luciano has most definitely chosen well.'

Celena did not know what to say. It was an extremely delicate situation. Giacoma was so proud, so happy, so pleased, with faint colour in her cheeks and a sparkle in her eyes. 'It was kind of you to let me wear your necklace and earrings.'

The woman frowned faintly. 'They are a gift; did not Luciano explain?'

Celena grimaced and nodded. 'But I couldn't possibly accept them; they're far too—'

'Nonsense,' cut in Giacoma peremptorily. 'My husband presented them to me on our engagement but I wear them no longer. I will be honoured if you wear them instead. It is right and fitting, as the future wife of my eldest great-grandson, that you should do so. The ring also was my engagement ring. Alas, I can no longer get it on my finger.'

'You could have it altered,' suggested Celena. 'Luciano can—'

'Don't argue, child.' It was an order, the old lady sitting up straight in her chair, her eyes piercing.

It was easy to see where Luciano got his authoritative ways from, thought Celena as she sat up a bit straighter herself. 'I'm sorry, and thank you. I will—always treasure them.' At least for as long as she continued to play the part.

'Now, Celena,' said Giacoma firmly, 'I think it is imperative that we start to make plans for your wedding. I am looking forward to meeting your sister, and if you have relatives, no matter how distant, they must come too.'

Celena was given no chance to speak; the old lady was in full flow, fired with enthusiasm, taking complete control. Celena wanted to tell her to stop, tell her that it was all a mistake, that Luciano was planning gain not happiness, that she didn't love him, that it was all a game, but how could she? How could she spoil this woman's pleasure? It would be such a body-blow to her that she would possibly never get over it. It would be up to Luc to do his own explaining, in such a way that his *bisnonna* wasn't hurt too much.

A quarter of an hour later the wedding was planned for a month's time and when Celena left Giacoma's room her head was spinning. She seemed to be getting deeper and deeper into something that she had wanted no part of in the first place. If only Luc hadn't take her passport; if only she could have gone back to England with him. If only, if only. . .

She had to escape, if merely for a few hours. Pausing just long enough to collect her handbag, Celena found her way out of the grounds and headed towards the town, not slowing her steps until she felt safely anonymous.

There she sauntered around Enna, admiring the various buildings, churches, shops, the enamelled pictures that decorated a tiled pavement, until finally, her feet aching, she sat down at a pavement café, and ordered herself a cup of coffee and a sandwich.

Absently she stirred the coffee. She had still not freed

her mind of the problems facing her. She still had to go back and listen to more of Great-grandmother's plans.

'I'm sure nothing can be that bad.'

The male voice penetrated her thoughts and she looked up with a swift frown, wondering if he could be talking to her. 'I beg your pardon?' He was dark and handsome, of medium build and around her own age.

'May I join you?' Without waiting for permission he slid into the seat opposite. 'Care to tell me about it?'

'How did you know I was English?' He had spoken with a heavy accent and although Celena resented his audacity she felt it would perhaps do her good to talk to someone else.

'You're certainly not Sicilian with hair that colour,' he told her, his brown eyes admiring, 'but I have to confess it was pure guesswork. What are you doing here all by yourself?'

'Thinking,' she told him.

'I can see that, but what deep, dark thoughts can possibly be troubling a beautiful girl like you? Are you on holiday?'

'Sort of,' she admitted.

'A mystery lady, no less.' He gesticulated for another coffee to be brought to their table. 'I am extremely curious. Start from the beginning and tell me everything.'

Little did he know how tempting that was, thought Celena.

'But, first of all, let me introduce myself. Raimondo Vittorini, owner of this salubrious establishment.' He held out his hand and Celena put hers into it.

'Celena Coulsden.' She withdrew her hand.

'Celena? A beautiful name for a beautiful lady.' His coffee arrived and he took a sip and then sat back. 'I am ready to hear this sad, sad story.'

He was mocking her, she knew, and yet it *was* sad, or

at least distressing. But it would be wrong to discuss it. Raimondo probably knew Luciano, or his family at least. She must be very careful what she said.

But before she could disclose anything Raimondo spoke again. 'Celena? Celena? I have heard that name before—recently. It has been on many people's lips. You are—' his eyes watched her carefully as he spoke '—Luciano Segurini's fiancée. Is that not so?'

Celena grimaced and nodded. She could not believe that it was already common knowledge.

'But if this is so then why the dismal face, and where is the proud man?'

'He was called back to England,' she admitted, 'on business.'

'Ah!' He spread his hands expressively. 'All is now clear. You are left alone in a strange country. Is it any wonder that you look so dejected? Please, it will be my pleasure to show you around our beautiful city. Luciano will not mind, I am sure.'

'I've already looked,' said Celena, shaking her head, 'but thank you for your offer, all the same.'

He sat talking to her for over half an hour, amusing her with various anecdotes and insisting on plying her with wine. By the time he reluctantly said he had things to do she was feeling much better. 'Thank you for entertaining me,' she said.

'At least you are now smiling, and I will be here tomorrow if you are still in need of stimulating company.' He took her hand and lifted it to his lips. '*Arrivederci*, Celena.'

When she arrived back at the villa Francesca was in a panic. 'Signor Segurini has been on the telephone,' she said rapidly in her native language. 'He was very angry because I could not find you.'

'It is not your fault, Francesca,' said Celena soothingly. 'I went for a walk and I was out longer than I expected. Do not worry; I will explain to him.'

'He said you should have told me.'

More than likely he was panicking because he thought she'd run away and spoilt everything, decided Celena. 'Is he ringing again?'

'Yet, *signorina*, in one hour.'

Perhaps, Celena thought wickedly, she ought to be out again. But she wasn't, and when she spoke to him she could not believe how angry he was.

'You went to Enna?' he enquired disbelievingly. 'Members of the Segurini family do not go wandering around alone in public.' He was at his most pompous. 'It is not safe.'

'What do you mean, not safe?' she asked. Surely he was attaching far too much importance to such a trifling event?

'Are you forgetting that the Segurinis are a very important family—almost akin to British royalty? You could have been kidnapped.'

Celena did not believe him for one moment. 'You're exaggerating,' she told him coldly. 'If there was that sort of danger you would have warned me.'

'I did not expect you to go wandering off alone,' he retorted.

'So I'm to thank my lucky stars that nothing happened, am I?' she questioned caustically. 'Thank you, Luc, but I am perfectly capable of looking after myself. I am not a member of your family; no one knows me; you're worrying for nothing.' She tried not to think about Raimondo and how easily he had placed her when she'd disclosed her name.

'May I ask why you felt it necessary to go out at all?'

Celena let out an impatient breath. 'Can't you guess? Sitting here on my own isn't much fun, especially with your great-grandmother making plans for our wedding.'

'She's doing that?' he asked in a complete change of voice.

'She's already done it,' retorted Celena savagely. 'One month's time, would you believe? I hadn't the heart to tell her I wouldn't be going through with it. That can be your pleasure.'

He was silent a moment before saying, 'We'll talk about it when I get back.' And the line went dead.

Celena stood holding the receiver for several seconds. What did he mean 'We'll talk'? Did he mean that he was going to do his utmost to persuade her to go through with the marriage ceremony? Was he serious? Was that truly his intention? Her heart thudded like a sledgehammer in her breast.

'Is there something wrong, *signorina*?' Francesca approached and looked at her worriedly.

Celena managed a faint smile. 'Not really.'

'Signor Segurini is still angry with you?'

'Just a little. I didn't realise that going out could cause so much trouble. Was Signora Segurini worried also?'

Francesca smiled. 'She does not know; she rarely leaves her room. But she is asking for you now.'

Celena felt impending disaster and wished there were some way she could avoid the meeting. If it was to discuss further wedding arrangements she would be tempted to blurt out the truth. Only two things would stop her—the shock to the old lady's system in her present state of health, and the fact that it would crucify her to know that her adored great-grandson was capable of such duplicity.

She really was in an impossible situation and with each hour that passed she hated Luciano more and more for getting her into it.

'Have you had your lunch, *signorina*?' Francesca's voice broke into her thoughts.

'Yes, thank you,' she answered. 'I hope it didn't inconvenience you?'

'It is all right,' said the girl. 'It was a cold meal anyway.'

Before answering her summons to the matriarch's room Celena took a shower and changed her dress. As usual, the imperative, '*Avanti!*' followed her tap on the door, and Giacoma sat in her red velvet chair, the blinds drawn, the room cool. None of the heat of the day was allowed to penetrate. Celena shivered.

'Sit down, child,' came the command after the customary kiss on the cheek.

Celena obediently lowered herself onto the carved wooden chair which was placed to the front and a little to one side of Signora Segurini. Everyone who came to see her had to sit there and Celena wondered whether they all felt as uncomfortable as she did.

'I have been drawing up a guest list, Celena, and I trust you have done the same?'

'Not yet,' she answered, startled. 'I went for a walk into Enna; I felt the need for some fresh air.'

'By yourself?' The old lady looked as scandalised as her great-grandson had sounded, and Celena knew immediately that she had said the wrong thing.

'It was an impulse,' defended Celena, 'and I was quite safe.'

'Maybe, but in future—' a warning finger wagged '—make sure that someone goes with you. Best of all, do not go out again until Luciano returns. You have plenty to do; there are many things to arrange. I have been on the telephone all morning and I am exhausted; I intend to take a sleep now, but this evening I want your list. Invitations have to be printed and sent out immediately.'

Giacoma seemed to have taken on a new lease of life. Celena was amazed at the keenness of her mind, and alarmed at the speed with which things were progressing.

The wedding, she discovered, was to take place in their own *cappella*, right here in the grounds; the reception would be in the ballroom, caterers were being brought in, flowers would be absolutely everywhere, and Giacoma's own seamstress was making the wedding dress.

When she was finally dismissed Celena went downstairs and out into the courtyard, pacing up and down, her mind totally confused. How had she got into this situation, for heaven's sake? And how was she going to get out of it without hurting Giacoma?

She headed towards the chapel and wandered inside. It was much bigger than she'd expected but what stunned her even more was its ornateness, the amount of gold treasure just sitting there, its overt declaration of wealth. None of this was repeated in the house, which was definitely in need of some money being spent on it.

Celena slid into a pew and sat down. She felt deathly cold and wrapped her arms about herself, and closed her eyes. One part of her said that she would be a fool to give up the chance of marrying such a wealthy man. She would be made for life; she would never want for anything as long as she lived.

Her other, more prosaic half told her that it wouldn't work, that love meant more than money. In any case, Luc had no intention of entering into a permanent arrangement. Once his great-grandmother left this earth and he took possession here she would have served her purpose. It would be the end, she would be released with a handsome pay-off and that would be that—so why marry him at all?

When she felt tears sliding down her cheeks Celena wondered why they were there, but it took several more, soul-searching minutes before the truth finally hit her—and she did not like what she found out.

It was not animal attraction she felt for Luc, not chemistry, not even hatred. It was something far more profound and disturbing—something she had never envisaged happening in a thousand years. In fact the unbelievable had taken place. She had incredibly, numbingly, horrifyingly fallen in love with him! It was the very worst possible scenario she could imagine, and yet it had happened, without her awareness, without her consent, without any warning at all.

CHAPTER SEVEN

CELENA dropped her head into her hands. How could she have fallen in love with a man like Luc? He was a man who had taken her life and turned it upside down, a man who had only one reason in mind for wanting to marry her—and it had nothing whatsoever to do with love.

How had it come about? Why? What had happened to all her vows? What had happened to her defensive wall? How had Luc managed to melt the ice that she had packed so tightly around her heart?

There was no answer to any of these questions. She felt totally confused and could not even begin to imagine what it would be like to marry a man she loved and then have that marriage revoked once she had served her purpose. There was no way she could go through with such a contract; it would be too devastating by far once she got her marching orders.

Luc would most definitely have to tell his great-grandmother that the engagement was off. With a bit of luck he would be back tomorrow—in any case he would return before the invitations were sent out—and in the meantime, much against her will, she would make her list, just to keep the old woman happy.

Worry kept Celena awake for most of the night. She had hoped in vain that Luc would ring again, and she'd fully intended making her feelings clear, but in the event it was late afternoon the next day before he returned.

She had had further discussions with Giacoma and

felt more and more trapped, and more and more uncomfortable about the whole thing, and now she was in such a state that the moment he walked into the house she went on the attack, completely ignoring the rush of warmth that assailed her, the fact that she now saw this man in an entirely new light.

'Luc, I refuse to play any further part in this farce. Your great-grandmother has completely taken over. I want to go home, and I want to go now.'

Luciano frowned at this sudden onslaught, and, dropping his case, he took her arm. 'Celena, calm down; I'm sure you're exaggerating.' He led her into his study, urging her down onto the burgundy leather chesterfield, pouring some brandy into a glass and pushing it into her hand.

Celena ignored the drink. 'I am not exaggerating,' she insisted. 'I've never known anything be organised so quickly. If I didn't know differently I'd think that you and she were in league.'

There were lines of strain on Luc's face; he had obviously been working hard and probably needed a rest, and in the light of her new-found feelings she felt desperately sorry for him. Nevertheless this thing had to be sorted out.

He sat beside her and she thought of the night of the party and what had happened then on this very settee, and she thought about the love running rampant through her body, but she squashed the thoughts immediately. Love had no part to play in any of this. She had to be ruled by her head, not her treacherous heart.

'Surely it's not too much to humour an old lady?' His tone was low but there was a hint of steel beneath the surface, and Celena knew that she had a battle on her hands.

'Humour her?' she asked, managing to inject some

indignation into her voice. 'Marriage isn't something to be entered into lightly, just to make someone happy. Marriage is sacred; it's a commitment between two people who love each other dearly and want to spend the rest of their lives together.' Not when only one person loved!

'I won't do it, I tell you,' she went on. 'I refuse to be used any longer. I insist, Luciano, that you tell her our engagement is over, that it's finished, that we've split up, that we've discovered we don't love each other— tell her anything, just as long as you put an end to it.'

His fingers tightened threateningly on hers. 'I somehow don't think that us not loving each other will be a problem. There is very definitely a strong physical attraction between us.' His voice deepened. 'It will—'

'It's not enough,' Celena interrupted sharply, but going through her mind was his suggestion that he was attracted to her too. Did it mean that his kisses weren't a deliberate part of the plan, that perhaps he hadn't been able to help himself? It was a startling thought and it caused her heart to race.

'I think it could be,' he said slowly. 'Many girls would give their right arm for such an opportunity.'

'But not this girl,' she cried in self-preservation. 'I suggest you renew your love affair with Simone; she would appear to be more than willing. Have you seen her again?'

'No, I haven't, as a matter of fact,' he answered. 'Would it bother you if I had?'

Celena shrugged. 'What you do is your own affair.'

But her tone was sharp and he smiled, as if sensing that Simone was a thorn in Celena's side. 'Let's not talk about Simone,' he said. 'Why don't you tell me what attributes a man would need before you felt you could marry him?'

Celena stamped on the fluttering of her heart. 'He'd need to be a saint,' she told him firmly.

An eyebrow quirked. 'A saint? There are not many of those about. I presume Andrew Holmes ran short of the mark?'

Celena's eyes shot wide. 'How do you know about him?'

Luc shrugged nonchalantly. 'Like I said when we first met, I know everything about you. I know that you went out with him for two years. I know that you were once engaged. What type of person was he?'

'Not the right type,' she retorted shortly. 'He two-timed me, rather devastatingly, and after that I decided on a career rather than marriage. So, you see, there is no way in the world you will persuade me to marry you.' Unless he declared that he loved her too—and there was no chance of that.'

'It would appear we have both had our disappointments,' he said gruffly. 'It creates a sort of bond, wouldn't you say?'

'No, I would not,' she returned fiercely.

'You wouldn't be hurt if you married me, Celena.' He took her hands in his, his thumbs beginning a slow massage. 'In fact it would be to your advantage.'

'Because I'd come out of it with a healthy bank balance?' she asked acidly. His insistent stroking was having a profound effect and when he raised his hands to touch her cheeks gently, when his palms felt warm and exciting and his brown velvet eyes locked into her own she felt waves of sensation flood through her.

How easy it would be to give in. All she had to do was close her eyes and pretend that he loved her too. There were times when she actually felt a rapport—and this was one of them, and it was dangerous—highly dangerous.

She wrenched away from him and stood up. 'You

won't get round me this way, Luciano,' she declared
bitterly. 'I've already made up my mind; nothing will
change it.'

Luc pushed himself slowly to his feet, unfolding
himself until he stood straight and tall in front of her.
Gone was the softness in his eyes, replaced by a
glittering anger. 'You may have some virtues, Celena,
but unselfishness isn't one of them.'

'You think I'm being selfish because I won't enter
into a—loveless marriage?' she asked crossly. 'If you
ask me it's you who—'

'I'm not talking about that,' he snarled. 'I'm talking
about my precious *bisnonna*. Would you really endan-
ger her health by walking out on me? Have you no
conscience?'

Celena swallowed hard. She had to admit that for the
moment she *had* forgotten about Giacoma; she *had*
been guilty of thinking only of herself, and the unhap-
piness such a marriage would cause.

'What's the matter?' he rasped. 'Have I hit a raw
spot?'

'Do you really think it would be the end of Giacoma
if I back out now?' she whispered in anguish.

He nodded grimly. 'I'm sure of it. She is fading fast;
the difference in her now and the last time I came is
unbelievable. She's a shadow of her former self.'

Celena closed her eyes and did a lot of soul-searching
and finally knew what her answer was going to be. She
had seen for herself how much this wedding meant to
Giacoma, what a difference it had made to her state of
mind. If she could give the woman a few months'
happiness, wouldn't that be better than totally destroy-
ing her? She had probably known all along that there
was no way out.

'Well, Celena, I am waiting.' He had drawn himself

up to his full height and there was no expression at all
on his handsome face.

She drew in an uneasy breath. 'I'll do it,' she said
huskily. 'But for Giacoma's sake, not yours. Don't
expect anything from me. It will be a marriage in name
only.' And it would crucify her in the light of her new
discovery.

The tension drained out of him. 'Thank you,' he said
simply. 'I'll make sure you don't regret it. Sicily is a
wonderful island; I think you'll enjoy living here.'

She frowned and looked at him sharply. 'You mean
we will be staying here permanently?' This was something that had never occurred to her, not even fleetingly.

He inclined his head.

'But your business. . .'

He gave a shrug. 'I think it's about time I eased up
on the reins and let Martin Thurslow take over. He's an
able man. Maybe in the beginning I'll need to commute,
but ultimately I plan to live here. This house has been
in our family for generations, and although it's been
neglected of late I intend restoring it to its former glory.
Rest assured, Celena, it will be like the palace it once
was when I've finished with it. You will be proud to be
part of our family.'

And this, she thought sadly, was what it was really all
about. This house, this family, the prestige of being its
head—it was all he wanted. He didn't care about his
great-grandmother, he didn't care about her, it was the
power he craved. How could she have forgotten that?

Her eyes suddenly flashed. 'Proud? I know why you
want to live here, Luciano Segurini, and it's not to
make your great-grandmother happy. You want to
become head of the family, you want to run the
household, but unless you're married Filippo will be the
one who succeeds. That's what the rush to get married

it all about, isn't it? Not for the sake of Giacoma's health.'

He looked stunned by her harsh words, a deep frown carving his brow, his eyes darkening. 'Where on earth have you heard this?'

'It's true, isn't it?' she insisted.

'It is true I will become head of the family, so to speak, yes,' he confessed darkly. 'But it is not true that it's the reason I want you to marry me. It is to make my beloved *bisnonna* happy, and—because—I am. . .' He paused and apparently had second thoughts about what he was going to say. 'Because I happen to think that it will work,' he finished hastily.

Celena's scepticism showed in her eyes.

'You don't believe me?' he barked. 'Who told you this nonsense?'

She lifted her shoulders. 'Does it really matter?'

'It matters a great deal,' he rasped, 'if someone's telling lies.'

'It was just something I—heard on the night of our engagement party,' she finally admitted.

He gave a bark of laughter. 'You shouldn't believe all you hear. People make things up; it's pure speculation, not a word of truth in it.'

How Celena would have loved to believe him.

'Enough of this nonsense,' he said brusquely. 'I'm going to shower and change before I see Bisnonna. First of all, though, I think it would be very right and proper to seal our bargain.'

His intention was clear and Celena backed, terrified now that she would give herself away. 'In name only were my terms,' she warned him.

'That is nonsense,' he said. 'You cannot put a barrier between us. What do you think the family will say?'

'They don't have to know,' she told him tightly. 'When they're around I'll act the part of the devoted fiancée; otherwise, don't expect anything.' And when he caught her shoulders in a punishing grip she added, 'It's either that or I get out of here now.'

Brown eyes glinted. 'Without your passport?'

She had forgotten that for the moment.

'And without any hope of finding another job?'

She glared.

'You'd force Davina out of boarding-school?' he taunted.

'You swine!' she spat, and then his mouth came down hard on hers.

The whole gamut of thundering emotions and sensations was triggered into life and there was nothing she could do to stop it. All that mattered was the here and now—Luc's kisses, his touch, his exciting body close to hers, the taste of him, the tantalising male smell of him. His kisses were like fire, searing and thrilling, burning and arousing, and subconsciously she urged her body closer to his.

Luc groaned and his arms about her tightened, and the kiss went on and on, his hands exploring, his body pulsing. Celena was beginning to wonder where it would end when amazingly he set her from him. 'I think that's enough—for now,' he said, and with a smile that looked very much like triumph he turned and left the room.

Why had she succumbed so easily? Celena asked herself. Why hadn't she contained her feelings? Thank goodness he hadn't guessed how she really felt; that would have been humiliation too deep to bear.

As things stood he would go on thinking that it was pure physical attraction. He would congratulate himself that he had found a girl capable of playing the part for as long as it took. Bitterness crept in as she thought of what he was doing to his *bisnonna*.

The woman would undoubtedly be pleased to see

him back; she probably knew already that he was here and would be expecting his visit. It was traditional to pay respect to the old lady in this manner, and on this occasion she would have much to tell him.

Celena took a walk in the grounds and did not see Luc again until they sat down to their evening meal, his brothers and sister and their respective spouses again joining them, their children already in bed. It seemed that his return was enough of a celebration to warrant them all eating together—all except Giacoma, who, as always, remained in her room.

The natural topic of conversation was their forthcoming wedding. Celena felt faintly uncomfortable but Luciano played his part magnificently, giving an excellent show of being in love with her.

He sat opposite, his eyes on her constantly, virtually making love to her, so that the colour rose in her cheeks and she could not help responding. Knowing that he was doing it purely for the benefit of his family made no difference. She reacted to him like a flower to the warmth of the sun.

And afterwards, when the others had returned to their own living quarters and she and Luciano were alone, he said, 'I'm glad you didn't let me down, Celena. You did well; no one would ever know that you don't love me. My *bisnonna* is deliriously happy too. I've never seen her like this. It makes it all worthwhile.'

She felt devastated. How could he sound so sincere when they both knew that his great-grandmother was of secondary importance? He was, sadly, a man she would never understand, nor ever trust, and if it hadn't been for a genuine compassion for Giacoma and concern for her sister's schooling she wouldn't have stayed here another minute.

'I'm glad you think so,' she said.

Luc frowned. 'Is something wrong? I thought everything was going particularly well.'

'I'm tired, that's all,' she lied, not wanting to get into another argument. It hurt her to fight with him. 'I think I'll go to bed.'

It was obvious from the sceptical lift of his eyebrows that he did not believe her, but he made no further comment, saying instead, 'A good idea; I'll join you. I've had a somewhat hectic day myself.'

As he accompanied her up the stairs Celena felt every nerve-end quiver in response to his male vibes; she could almost feel the heat of his body, and she desperately hoped that he would take her into his arms and give her a long, lingering goodnight kiss.

When all he did was place a perfunctory kiss on her brow before carrying on to his own room she experienced the bitter sting of tears. What more proof did she need that she was a commodity to be used only when necessary?

The fact that she had herself declared that she would play-act only in front of the others escaped her and she began to have second thoughts about the wisdom of agreeing to marry Luc. She could be heading for more heartache than she was able to handle.

However, when the dressmaker came the next morning she knew it was too late to back out. In front of Giacoma styles and fabrics were discussed, measurements taken, and she had very little say in any of it.

In one way it suited her; it was best to let everything flow over her head and not get too deeply involved. She pretended that it was happening to someone else, that it was something she was watching from afar, something that had nothing to do with her.

Luc's nephews and nieces, who were to be page-boys and bridesmaids, were all highly excited, running around the house with great smiles on their faces—and it seemed that everyone was happy but herself.

Having absented himself while all this was taking place, Luc was in a thunderous mood when he returned. He sought Celena out, gripping her arm so tightly that it hurt, virtually frogmarching her into his study. 'I have just heard something that distresses me deeply.' His eyes were cold and accusing, almost black in their intensity.

'Oh?' Celena frowned, having no idea at all what he was talking about.

'Does the name Raimondo Vittorini mean anything to you?'

Celena smiled. 'Of course. He is the proprietor of—'

'Exactly,' he cut in swiftly, 'and I want to know what you were doing with him.'

She looked at him in open-mouthed astonishment. 'What do you mean, what was I doing? I was doing nothing—except drinking coffee and talking.'

'And partaking of wine, I believe,' he added coldly. 'And more than talking—a kiss, I understand, took place.'

His arrogance and total aggression were unbelievable. Celena shook her head in disbelief. 'This is ridiculous,' she protested. 'Who told you?'

'I don't think that matters,' he retorted harshly and coldly. 'The point is that you are betrothed to me. If this is the sort of thing that happens when you go out alone then I am glad I have forbidden it. I will not have the Segurini name besmirched.'

Celena gasped. He surely couldn't be serious? 'Raimondo was merely being polite; he was trying to cheer me up as a matter of fact. I was unhappy because you had gone back to England. If it's anyone's fault I was out alone it's yours,' she added fiercely.

'From what I hear it was more than politeness.'

'Then you heard wrong,' she snapped. 'Whoever your informant is they're out to cause trouble.' And he or she was succeeding! 'It was an entirely innocent conversation. Besides, Raimondo told me that he knew you. He would hardly proposition me under those circumstances. He was very much a gentleman. The kiss was on my hand—a goodbye kiss, nothing more.' She was truly indignant and rose to her feet but he pushed her mercilessly back down.

'The Segurinis have a very high reputation,' he declared tightly. 'I do not wish it to be blemished by thoughtless and irresponsible acts.'

Celena's eyes flashed her fury, all thoughts of love forgotten at this moment in time. 'I think you are overreacting, I think you are being ridiculous, and if this is what things are going to be like then you can forget the wedding; I want none of it. I'm going to pack right this minute and go home.'

CHAPTER EIGHT

LUCIANO'S iron hand fell on Celena's shoulder as she again got to her feet. 'You're going nowhere, Celena. Stop being melodramatic.'

'You mean you'll hang onto my passport and credit cards until it suits your purpose to let me go?' she questioned tartly. 'I suppose you also know that I don't have very much cash—certainly not enough to get me home. Are you going to keep me short of that as well? Am I being kept prisoner?'

His sigh was deep and impatient. 'Not a prisoner in the true sense of the word, but surely you can understand my distress when I heard that you had been seen out with another man?'

She looked at him coldly. 'Maybe you should have asked for *my* version first, before going off at the deep end.'

'Whatever your excuse,' he said in an equally icy voice, 'it was unwise of you to go out alone under the circumstances. However, I am prepared to overlook it this once. Consider the matter closed.'

Celena could not believe his attitude. Anyone would have thought that he was already head of the Segurini family. This imperiousness, this overbearing arrogance were obviously bred into him from a very early age. Thank goodness, she thought, that she wasn't entering into a permanent relationship. Love him or not, she could never have put up with such unreasonable restrictions.

* * *

108

Throughout the next month Celena felt as though her life had been taken over; every decision was made for her and she was expected to agree without question. Replies to the invitations had flooded in but apart from her sister, who had expressed great delight upon hearing the news, no other members of her family were able to make it. The rest of the hundred or so guests would all be on Luciano's side.

She would never have been able to go through with it if she had not loved him, Celena decided after one particularly trying session with Giacoma. Despite Luciano's claims that the woman was fading quickly, she seemed to have found great resources of energy, and her mind and memory were razor-sharp.

When Luciano announced that he had to make yet another visit to England, to install Martin officially as his manager, Celena again declared that she wanted to go with him. 'I need my clothes, and I suppose I shall have to sell my house, or at the very least rent it out long-term. There are lots of loose ends I need to tie up.'

But once more Luciano was adamant. 'You absolutely cannot—there is far too much to do here; you must help Bisnonna, and I'm sure you must still have dress fittings and all manner of things to do. Give me your key and make a list and I will see to everything for you.'

And no matter how she argued he would not change his mind. She privately thought that he was being most unfair—unless there was some other reason he did not want her to go with him. Like another woman for instance. Like Simone!

She must have left the island by now. It was strange that she hadn't put in another appearance. She had been so adamant about wanting to get back with Luc and yet here they were with the wedding only days away and Simone had done nothing to try and stop it.

When her sister arrived the day before the wedding, feeling important because she had travelled all this way alone, and terribly excited by the event that was about to take place, Celena hadn't the heart to tell her that it wasn't a love-match. Davina thought Luciano was a dream.

'I envy you, Lena,' she said, sitting cross-legged on the bed in Celena's room. 'I hope I meet a man like him one day.' She rolled her eyes skywards. 'Even his name sounds romantic. And this house—is this where you're going to live?'

Celena nodded.

'It's magnificent, isn't it? Do you have your own maid?' Davina's eyes were saucer-wide.

'No,' replied Celena with some amusement. 'There's only Francesca, who does most of the cleaning and general duties; her mother is cook-cum-housekeeper, and her father does the garden. I don't think the Segurinis are as rich as they look, although they're a very noble family. I suppose they used to have money, and Luc's certainly very wealthy in his own right. His brothers and sister live here also, in their own apartments.'

'So it won't be just the two of you?'

'Heavens, no!' exclaimed Celena. 'There's Great-grandmother as well; Luc adores her.'

'I didn't realise,' said Davina. 'Perhaps it won't be so much fun after all.'

'We'll have our own rooms and Luc wants to do the place up,' explained Celena, 'so there'll be plenty to keep me occupied. And of course you'll come and stay in your school holidays.'

Davina wrinkled her nose. 'But it won't be *yours*, will it? It won't be the same. When I get married I want to be totally alone with my husband.'

Celena privately agreed and thought it about time

she changed the subject. 'Tell me about school. Is your friend Louise still there?'

'She certainly is,' said Davina, 'and we both agree it's the best school ever.'

'And how are your grades these days?' There had been a worrying time after their parents had died when Davina did not do very well.

The younger girl grinned. 'I'm top in almost everything. Mum and Dad would be so proud of me.'

Celena hugged her. 'I know they would, and *I* am proud of you. You're the best sister ever.' Seeing how happy Davina was, hearing how well she was doing, Celena knew that she had made the right decision. No matter how hard things got, it would be worth it in the long run.

The big day dawned and the *cappella* overflowed. The solemn ceremony seemed to take for ever and Celena again felt as though it was happening to someone else. She was not aware of very much except Luc at her side—handsome Luc in a dark suit, smiling tenderly, squeezing her hand when she appeared nervous, as attentive as any bridegroom could be. He played the part to perfection, giving every impression of being deeply in love with her.

The whole day passed in a haze. Congratulations came from all sides, speeches were made, mountains of food were consumed, and there was dancing, drinking, talking, laughing. She was the constant focus of attention and Giacoma presided over it all like a queen.

Celena felt relief when the day finally came to an end, when their guests left and only Davina, who was going back to England the next day, remained. And even her sister had gone to bed when she and Luc finally climbed the stairs.

Celena was apprehensive. It was their own apartment

in the west wing that she was going to now, Luc's bedroom she was sharing tonight—and every night until he decided that she had served her purpose. If this disquieting thought hadn't been at the forefront of her mind, if Luc had loved her too instead of merely desiring her, she would have been the happiest girl in the world; as it was, her heart was as heavy as lead.

There was to be no honeymoon; they were staying here in this house, with his family and his great-grandmother, and he would pretend to be in love with her and she would act the dutiful part of the happy wife—in front of his relatives—but she was determined not to sleep with him.

Once in his bedroom, however, once he had closed the door, he turned and took her into his arms. 'My magnificent Celena,' he said. 'You were wonderful today.'

Contact was electric and it was all she could do to say coldly, 'Was I? I actually felt an imposter.'

His arms tightened. 'You behaved beautifully; I'm proud of you—and my *bisnonna* adores you. At last she is content.'

Celena privately wondered whether Giacoma ever would be satisfied. There had been veiled suggestions about starting a family straight away. And she wished that Luc wouldn't keep going on about his great-grandmother's happiness when she knew it was the position as head of the family that he coveted above everything else. Hadn't his brother said more or less the same thing when she'd been talking to him the other day?

'Of course Luciano always had to be top dog,' Filippo had said with a wry attempt at humour, 'even when we were children. There was always a lot of good-natured rivalry between us. I take it he's told you that he won't inherit the title if he's not married?'

Celena had nodded. 'Something along those lines.' And she had felt sickened to the core. This was conclusive proof that Simone's warning hadn't been without truth, however much Luc might deny it.

Filippo had laughed. 'I sometimes privately thought he'd get married just to spite me, but I was wrong. It's clear to everyone that he's head-over-heels in love with you.'

Celena had grimaced. It just went to prove what a good actor Luciano was.

'And do you know what?' Filippo had gone on. 'I'm glad he's getting married because I didn't really want to be head of the family. It's a tremendous responsibility; I don't think I could handle it.'

Celena had been able to understand his relief. Filippo was quieter than Luc, less assertive, and was happy to lead his own life without worrying about others.

Luc's voice dragged her back to the present. 'You've been driving me crazy all day, Celena,' he declared thickly. 'I count myself incredibly lucky in having found someone like you.'

She jerked herself free. 'It's worked out very well for you, hasn't it?'

He frowned, seeming surprised by her sudden sharp words. 'Celena, what is wrong?'

'What is wrong?' she echoed coldly. 'Your constant reminders that I'm here to serve a purpose is what is wrong.' And the fact that she loved him and couldn't tell him. It was driving her insane.

There were sudden taut lines about his mouth and eyes. 'You're being unreasonable.'

'I don't think so,' she retorted. 'You lose no opportunity in pointing out that I'm here at your bidding only. Well, maybe I am, maybe you have bought me, but, as I said before, our love affair is for public eyes only. In private keep your rotten hands off me.'

'Celena, you can't mean that.' He attempted to take her into his arms again. 'You're tired; it's been a long day; you—'

'I know what I am saying.' She ripped herself away from him, her eyes a stormy grey.

'You are being unreasonable,' he said, anger growing inside him now.

'Am I?' she demanded, drawing herself up haughtily and glaring at him.

'Yes, you are. All day you've given every appearance of being happy. If I didn't know better I would have said that you had fallen in love with me.'

'In love with *you*?' Horror that she had given herself away made Celena's voice shrill. 'How could I be in love with a man who *uses* me? All I'm guilty of, Luc, is feeling a physical attraction—and I deeply regret that. If there was something I could do about it I would.'

His mouth tightened at her sharp words. 'I'm sorry you feel that way.'

'And so am I,' she retorted. 'So am I.'

'You knew all along the reason I wanted to marry you and you seemed happy to go along with it. Why the sudden change of heart now? Of all the times you could pick to—'

'There's no change,' she told him acidly. 'I never agreed that I would sleep with you. I guess I'm not like other women you've met. I imagine none of them ever refused to go to bed with you. I'm sorry if I don't conform but—'

It was his turn to interrupt. 'To set the matter straight, I do not bed every woman I meet.'

'Not even when they throw themselves at you?'

'More especially not then,' he replied tersely. 'I happen to be very selective.'

Her eyes flashed. 'Should I be honoured that you *selected* me?'

'This is no time for being facetious,' he barked.

'But it is time for bed. Goodnight, Luc.' She turned to open the door, fully intending to go to her old room, but he was up like a shot, his hand firm on her shoulder, propelling her back inside.

'*This* is where you are sleeping,' he grated. 'You're to do nothing that will give rise to wagging tongues.'

'You should have thought of that before making your plans,' she tossed back furiously. The trouble was that she *did* want to sleep with Luc; she ached for him; her whole body cried out for him. She just hated the thought that all Luc would be doing was satisfying his male urges.

'Nevertheless you are sleeping in my bed,' he announced, and the hard lines on his face brooked no refusal. 'If it is your wish, I will not touch you, but you are not setting foot outside this room.'

'Very well.' Celena kept her chin high as she opened a drawer and plucked out a nightdress that Francesca had carefully placed there earlier, and then she marched across with it to the adjoining bathroom.

Luciano's harsh voice rent the air. 'What do you think you are doing?'

She turned and eyed him coldly. 'What does it look like?'

'It looks as though you're afraid to let me see you get undressed.'

Her eyes flashed. 'Not afraid of you looking at me, Luc, simply ensuring you don't take advantage.' In truth it was self-preservation. No matter how angry she got, the need in her body remained, and if he so much as came near her there was a very grave danger that she would give herself to him.

He let out a hiss of anger, his nostrils flaring. 'Whatever else I might be, I am not a lecher. Now get undressed and stop being foolish.'

Celena had changed out of her wedding dress earlier in the evening and was now wearing a high-necked silk brocade sheath in ivory shot through with gold, made also by Giacoma's dressmaker. It was exquisite, by far the most beautiful dress she had ever owned, but—and she had forgotten this until now—it fastened all the way down the back with tiny pearl buttons. There was no way she could get out of it without Luc's help.

She tossed her nightdress onto the bed and quietly and reluctantly said, 'I think I might need your help.'

His mouth curved into a smile, all the anger draining out of him. 'Poor Celena. How difficult it must be for you to ask.'

Don't mock me, she wanted to cry out, but she kept silent, simply turning her back to him, tensing as she felt his fingers brush her neck.

'Relax; I'm not going to molest you,' he growled.

It took him ages to undo the first tiny button; he seemed to have difficulty with the delicately embroidered loop—no doubt because of his big male hands, or because he wanted the task to last, she decided, because he was enjoying it, because he wanted to torment her! He knew how little control she had over her body where he was concerned.

Davina had fastened the dress up for her earlier, and she had done it in no time, seeming to have no trouble at all.

Button two was undone and the torture continued. Buttons three and four followed and there were still only two inches of dress open. 'How long is it going to take?' she asked, shocked to hear the huskiness in her voice.

'I guess all night,' he answered, and there was roughness in his tone also.

'If I thought you meant that, Luciano Segurini,' she retorted smartly, 'I would fetch my sister to do it; her fingers are much nimbler than yours. I suspect that you're deliberately taking your time.'

'It's a very pleasurable task,' he agreed. 'There, that's another one. I wonder if whoever made this dress knew what they were doing?'

'It was designed by your great-grandmother and made by her seamstress,' Celena told him. 'It never occurred to me that I'd have this trouble with it.'

'My *bisnonna*, eh?' And there was a smile in his voice. 'I might have known. She's an incurable romantic.'

Celena jerked her head round to look at him. 'You think she deliberately had it made this way, knowing that I'd have to ask you to undo it?'

'Undoubtedly.' He grinned. 'She's probably envisaging this scene right now.'

'I don't believe it,' said Celena huffily.

'I think you should,' he muttered, and when the next couple of buttons came undone he pressed his lips to the warm, scented skin of her nape.

Celena flinched at the unexpectedness of his kiss and wanted to tear herself away but could not move. His hands stroked the soft flesh of her upper arms and all she wanted was for him to make love to her. But what she wanted and what she deemed sensible were two different things. 'Have you forgotten what you're supposed to be doing?' she asked sharply.

'I find this much more interesting,' he growled, his breath warm and exciting on her throat.

'Maybe, but I insist that you get on with the job,' she retorted.

'All in good time, Celena.' His mouth continued to assault, to slide over the slender column of her throat, to nibble the incredibly erotic area behind her ears. And then another button was undone, and each one after that was accompanied by a kiss, grazing over her skin, sending treacherous need through the very heart of her.

Before he had finished she would be his to do with as he liked, and she guessed that he knew it, that this was his intention. But, as there still weren't enough buttons undone for her to step out of the dress, unless she ripped it apart she was at his mercy.

It was open nearly to her waist now and the torment in her body was almost out of control. His hands moved excruciatingly over her slender back, his tongue tasting her delicately perfumed skin, teeth grazing her as he insidiously slid the exquisite material from her shoulders.

It was an agony of pleasure and Celena hated herself for allowing it, but she had long since lost the strength to move. Subtle shaping had been moulded into the dress so that it needed no bra, and when her aching curves were exposed, when he took their fullness into his palms, when his thumbs brushed over her tender pink nipples she gasped out aloud and, twisting around, offered her mouth up for his kiss.

Deep, pagan hunger gnawed away inside her, moist lips were parted and she no longer had any thoughts of sleeping in separate beds. Luc excited her like no other man ever had and she felt a desperate need to be possessed by him.

To her chagrin he did no more than lightly feather her lips before turning her back again. 'There's no rush, my sweetheart,' he whispered gruffly. 'We have all the time in the world.'

She thought he would carry on with the task of unbuttoning her dress but instead he continued to assault her aching breasts, to tease and torment her tingling, sensitive nipples, to nibble her throat as though he were a man dying of hunger. Did he know that he was driving her insane?

'You are so beautiful, my darling wife.'

Pressed back against him, Celena could feel his own deep arousal and marvelled that he had the strength to take things so slowly.

A few more buttons were undone until finally he was able to slide the heavy silken material over her hips. It fell to the floor and Celena stepped out of it. And then he turned her to face him.

All she wore was a scrap of lace and her high heels, but she felt no shame or embarrassment. In fact Luc's eyes roving over the full length of her body added to her excitement. Every inch of her was sensitised and her hips moved in tiny involuntary gestures which did not escape his notice.

'Undress me,' he commanded in a thick, guttural voice that sounded entirely unlike his own.

Celena had never undressed a man before and she was unsure where to start, unsure really whether she wanted to. But the thought, once it had taken hold, was vastly exciting, and she stepped closer to him, first of all slipping the knot in his tie and lifting it from around his neck, but her fingers trembled when she tried to slot the buttons of his shirt through their buttonholes. Was this the reason it had taken him so long? she wondered. Had he been equally disturbed and excited?

She dared not look at his face, though the intoxicating smell of sexy male animal drugged her senses like nothing else could, and the heat from his body was like a furnace. Her palms were moist by the time she had finished unbuttoning his shirt and had exposed the tanned, hard magnificence of his chest.

It was instinctive to touch him, to trace her fingers over his hair-roughened skin, to feel powerful muscle beneath her palms, and the unsteady thump of his heart! She wanted to brush her breasts against him but somehow did not quite dare.

She had difficulty with the clip on his trousers, and sliding down the zip caused a further heat through her loins. She pulled the fine linen down over his lean, narrow hips and felt her own heart boom within her breast. Down the length of his legs they went—but she had forgotten about his shoes.

'Will you—please—sit down?' she asked, her mouth so dry that speaking was difficult.

Not once had she looked into his eyes but now she dared to do so and felt a fresh surge through her limbs at the glazed look of desire, at the hunger and passion and totally desperate need. Whatever else their marriage might lack it certainly wasn't this.

She pulled off each handmade leather shoe in turn, his black silk socks, and finally his trousers, until all he was left in was a pair of very brief white pants, which hid none of his masculinity.

He stood and held out his arms and Celena went unhesitatingly into them. 'Do you still want to sleep in separate beds?' he asked huskily.

She shook her head.

He groaned and pulled her hard against him, his mouth seeking hers, his kiss more anguished and searching and probing than any other he had given her. Her own response too was total. There was no holding back now.

She was lifted effortlessly and carried to the bed; he eased her minuscule white lace briefs down over her hips and discarded his own pants too—and then he lay beside her, his arm over her body, his velvety brown eyes looking into hers, and his expression was tender and loving and if Celena had not known better she would have been convinced that he loved her.

What happened after that was like a dream—a long, beautiful dream in which she was transported into a world where touch and sensations and excitement beyond measure were paramount.

She was aware of him kissing and touching and stroking every single inch of her, conscious of the slow thoroughness of his lovemaking, conscious too that she was responding in like manner; but, as on previous occasions, it was as though it wasn't her doing these things, it wasn't her feeling this unutterable excitement, it was someone else and she was a bystander, watching this glorious experience unfold before her eyes.

It was a strange, unique feeling, and when finally, after what seemed like hours and hours of exquisite arousal, he entered her body, Celena lifted herself to him, at last realising that this was actually happening to her.

Her nails dug into his back as she arched her body to welcome each thrust. It was what she had ached and longed for ever since her discovery that she was in love with Luc, and for the moment she forgot that he did not love her. All she knew was that he was taking her to heights never reached before. If this was what being married to Luc meant then she had no regrets.

His breathing was rapid now—short, rasping gasps— his movements more and more urgent, until at last, when she felt that her own release was imminent, he shuddered violently and cried out as his body ultimately surrendered to hers.

It was sweet, sweet capitulation. Celena had never been conscious of such intensified feelings, never felt such spiralling esctasy; she felt at one with Luc, and when he rolled onto his side she still clung, and he held her, and there wasn't an inch of space between their bodies. In the long silence that followed they both still felt the need for togetherness.

She and Andrew had made love but it had never, ever reached such heights; she had never felt this wondrous elevation, this feeling of being a part of her mate, that they were two halves who had come together because of some predestined fate.

Even now faint tremors still thrilled through her body, and she urged herself even closer towards him. Luc groaned and held her with arms of steel and during the night they made love again and again.

Come morning Celena felt like a woman reborn, she felt glowing and beautiful and utterly, deliciously feminine. She spent a few moments looking at the sleeping Luc at her side, touching his shoulder gently with her fingertips, bending to press a kiss to his brow before sliding quietly out of bed.

Her reflection in the bathroom mirror confirmed her feelings. Her eyes sparkled, her skin glowed and she looked what she felt—a woman well and truly in love.

When she returned Luc was sitting up, his eyes devouring her, and Celena was no longer self-conscious about her nakedness; in fact she felt good about it, her eyes bright with the confidence of knowing that she had the ability to arouse this man to such heights.

OK, he wasn't in love with her—she didn't believe he was for one minute despite what Filippo had said—but he was a magnificent lover and she would be well provided for; what else mattered under the circumstances? She would not let herself think any further.

'Celena, you are surely the most beautiful woman in the whole world.'

She smiled and crept back into bed, snuggling up against him, enjoying the exciting warmth of his body. His hand possessively cupped and stroked a breast and Celena was just wondering whether she could survive another bout of lovemaking when a tap came on their door.

'I asked Francesca to bring us our breakfast in bed,' he admitted ruefully. 'I guess the timing's out.'

Celena slid down between the sheets as he called the girl in, and Francesca shyly set the tray down on the dressing table and scuttled back out with averted eyes.

Luc grinned as he fetched the tray and settled it down between them, and there, as naked as the day they were born, they sipped freshly squeezed orange juice, Luc fed her thin slices of toast smothered with lime marmalade, and they drank Earl Grey tea, which was a favourite of his.

It was a splendid breakfast, quite the nicest Celena had ever tasted, and afterwards they slid back between the sheets and Celena felt happier than she had in her whole life.

It was with reluctance that he finally declared that they ought to get up. 'I could spend the rest of my life making love to you,' he said with a smile that melted her heart.

The next week was one of the happiest that Celena had ever spent. Luc gave her his full attention, taking her out and showing her his beloved island, treating her as though she were indeed the love of his life.

Until the day came when he announced that he needed to go to England yet again to sort out a few further business matters. Celena smiled radiantly. 'Good. I can come with you this time.' There was nothing to stop her now. 'I can check up on my house.'

Although she would have preferred to rent it out, so that she would have somewhere to go back to when her marriage came to an end, Luc had actually put it on the market.

To her utter amazement he would not hear of her accompanying him. 'I shall be far too busy for you; it is much better that you stay here. Why don't you use the time to plan how you would like our rooms refurbished? Isn't that something all women love?'

But Celena did not want to stay. 'I don't mind if you're busy,' she said urgently. 'There are plenty of things I can do. Furniture to be got rid of.' Or put into store! That would probably be the best plan, she thought. 'I need to—'

'*This* is your home now, Celena,' Luc cut in brutally, 'and this is where you are staying.'

CHAPTER NINE

CELENA found it difficult to understand why Luc was being so obstinate. Her eyes flashed. 'Perhaps there's another reason you don't want me with you?' she suggested passionately. 'A certain person by the name of Simone? Could she be the reason you keep darting backwards and forwards?'

Luc surprisingly smiled. 'How you love to bring Simone's name into the conversation. If I didn't know better I would say you were jealous.'

'Jealous!' she echoed, wishing it weren't true. 'Why should I be jealous?'

'You tell me,' he said.

'It's nonsense—I'm not. It's just strange, that's all, that you keep flying out to England and yet you won't take me with you.'

'I just don't see any point when there's so much to be done here,' he said reasonably. 'I will obviously check if there's any mail for you, and I'll see the estate agents too, but everything else I have organised. It is all done for you.'

Celena had no doubt that she would enjoy planning the refurbishment of their apartment; it certainly needed doing. The curtains were dingy and almost threadbare, as was the carpet, and the wallcoverings looked as though they had been there since the year dot. But she would have much rather gone with Luc. There was surely no urgency?

She glared her resentment and tried again but he was adamant, and in the end she was forced to admit defeat.

125

'It looks as though again I have no choice,' she commented bitterly.

Luc smiled faintly and Celena fancied that his look was tinged with triumph; then he took her into his arms. 'I knew you'd see sense, my beautiful wife.' And as he kissed her he drugged her senses, and Celena knew that whatever he asked she would always do. Somehow, some way, she had fallen under his spell.

He left early the next morning, after a night of lovemaking that—for her—had been as tender as it had been meaningful. The initial urgency on their wedding night, the initial animal hunger had gone, and he'd taken his time and taught her an awareness of her own body that she'd never known, and she'd learned about his too—and the intimacy and the sensuality and the absolute togetherness had made everything else bearable. Those moments alone had more than made up for the pressure he had put her under.

When she told Giacoma, on her now ritual morning visit to the old lady's room, that she intended going into either Catania or Palermo to pick up samples of wallcoverings and swatches of materials the woman was shocked to the core and would hear none of it.

Celena had thought that telling Luc's great-grandmother her plans was simply a matter of courtesy; she had not thought for one moment that the woman would expressly forbid them. It was a different thing altogether from wandering around their local village on her own; she would be completely anonymous. And as there was a spare car in the garage what was the problem?

'It was Luc's suggestion that I spend my time planning the refurbishment of our rooms while he is away,' she protested faintly, not wishing to offend the old lady too much. 'I'm sure he didn't—'

'Did he also suggest that you go around looking for samples when the obvious thing is to have them sent here?' cut in the woman, her tone sharp.

Celena shrugged. 'Well, not exactly, but I don't see why I can't.'

'It is not the Segurini way,' announced Giacoma haughtily. 'I will give you lists of people whom you can contact. Samples, catalogues—anything you want—can be delivered here. Tell them who you are and they will be with you this afternoon.'

'I really don't think it's necessary,' said Celena, feeling a very real need to fight on this issue; otherwise she would never be allowed to do a thing for herself. It would be worse than purgatory, being tied to this house twenty-four hours a day. 'In any case, I need to get my hair cut. I thought I'd—'

Giacoma's many-ringed hand lifted, instantly stopping Celena's words. 'My own hairdresser will attend to your needs. I will ring her immediately and arrange for her to come.' And then she smiled, as though realising that she was being too officious, and said softly, 'I am aware that our ways are different from yours, Celena, and that it will, perhaps, take a little time for you to adjust, but running around doing things for yourself will not do at all.'

Celena privately thought that they were outdated views but she did not want to upset Giacoma. When Luc returned, however, she fully intended voicing her opinion, insisting that she be given some freedom. She could not see why going out by herself would do the Segurini reputation any harm, and his talk about being kidnapped was laughable. It was not as if anyone knew her—not yet; she was too new to this island.

She eventually made her phone calls and the various samples duly arrived but Celena had lost all enthusiasm. She left them on the table in their sitting room and read a book instead, but even then she was unable to concentrate. Luc had bullied her into a totally unreal situation and if she had had any inkling of what was in store she would never have taken up his job offer in the first place.

He rang her that evening but she did not think that this was an issue they could discuss over the telephone so she pretended that nothing was wrong.

'I'm missing you,' he growled.

Missing making love to her more likely, thought Celena bitterly. It was the only good part about their marriage.

'Think of me a little in bed tonight.'

'I'll try,' she whispered, surprised to feel her own passion rising at the sound of his voice. Where was the anger that had raged all day?

'Are you all right, Celena?'

'Yes,' she said faintly.

'Missing me too?'

'Mmm.'

He chuckled. 'Is that a yes or a no?'

'It's a yes,' she said huskily. After her visit to Giacoma that morning she had seen no one all day except Francesca, and had never felt so alienated in her whole life.

'I'll be back tomorrow,' he promised.

'I'm looking forward to it,' she said.

Another throaty chuckle. 'That sounds promising.'

'What are you doing now?' Celena asked.

'I'm ready to go out to dinner—with Martin and his wife,' he added pointedly. Then, on a harder note, he said, 'I trust you've not seen Raimondo again in my absence?'

'I've not been out,' she announced, and her tone was slightly harder too, but he did not seem to notice.

'I'm glad you're settling in,' was all he said.

Afterwards Celena wondered how he could be so singularly insensitive to her needs. Did he really think that she would be happy imprisoned in this house for day after long day, that she would be happy organising redecorations? Did he not think that she desired the company of others, that she needed something more to tax her brain? With the car advertisement out of the way there was absolutely nothing left for her to do.

She was used to a busy office atmosphere, to using her intelligence for something more useful than selecting the right colours and materials to go together. And how often was he going to be away? She could not see Luc stagnating in this big house. He was a high-powered business executive; he couldn't just sit here and do nothing except be lord of the manor. They had a lot of talking to do.

It was lonely in bed that night; during the last week she had got used to sleeping with Luc, could not imagine it any other way now. In this respect they were completely compatible and she was very much looking forward to his return.

She still could not altogether see why they had to live here when his business interests lay in England. He would never give up the advertising agency completely, even though Martin was eminently capable of running Luse. It was Luc's baby, and he was proving how difficult it was for him to let go by running backwards and forwards so frequently.

If he really wanted to live in Sicily but felt it necessary to keep in close touch with London, why didn't he have a computer link-up from here? Or would Great-grandmother throw her hands up in horror at the thought of such modern technology in her house?

It was almost a wonder that they had a telephone, thought Celena wryly. Giacoma definitely still lived in

the nineteenth century. But if Luc thought that his new
wife was going to conform without a fight he was very
much mistaken.

He had not said what time he would be home and
Celena waited impatiently the next day. She still could
not whip up any enthusiasm for wallpapers and paints
and took a walk in the garden instead. How she would
have loved to go into Enna and wander around on her
own. The restrictions were proving very burdensome
and the longer they were imposed, the more irritable
she got.

Just before lunch, as she was heading back towards
the house, the sound of a vehicle approaching made her
pulses quicken, though they subsided instantly when it
was not Luc's Mercedes that pulled up but a well-
polished red Fiat—and who should get out of it but
Simone! So she wasn't in England! The thought gave
Celena little satisfaction.

The girl wore a white, low-cut, figure-hugging dress,
teamed with red high-heeled sandals and belt, and
vibrant matching nail polish. Was it a coincidence that
the car was red too? wondered Celena as she frowned
her surprise.

In the clear light of day she could see that any
resemblance between the two of them was purely
superficial. And as she got nearer to the other girl she
saw that her eyes were a cat-like green and not grey
like her own. 'I thought you had gone back to England,'
she said bluntly.

The girl's fine brows lifted. 'You obviously thought
wrong. He took me with him the last time he went—I
expect he told you—but not on this occasion. Is he back
yet?'

Her words stopped the breath in Celena's throat.
Simone had been to England with Luc—and yet he

wouldn't take his own wife! Fury washed over her like a sudden rain squall. He had dared to ask her if she had seen Raimondo, and yet he had been dating Simone!

Why the hell had she fallen for such a devious swine? Why had she let him bully her into this sham of a marriage? He was everything she hated in a man, everything she had learned to distrust, and the sooner she was out of here the better.

Celena eyed the girl coldly. 'No, he isn't.' Her own blue and mauve dress made less of a statement but was nevertheless intensely feminine, with a floaty, layered skirt and a pretty scalloped neckline. She felt good in it and certainly had no intention of letting Simone see that she was upset. 'Is he expecting you?'

Green eyes flashed. 'I don't have to make an appointment to see Luciano.'

'Perhaps you should.' Celena allowed herself a faint smile. 'He's a very busy man.'

'As if I didn't know,' sighed Simone delicately. 'I don't see half as much of him as I would like. What time will he be here?'

'I'm not sure,' Celena answered coolly.

Simone smiled evilly. 'Now that is interesting. He hasn't let his own wife know when he will be home. It certainly proves one thing, doesn't it?'

With a questioning lift of her brows Celena waited.

'It proves that he doesn't love you.' The girl's eyes were alight with cruel intent. 'He wouldn't leave you alone like this if he did. I was right—he did marry you because of his inheritance. And if it hadn't taken me so long to come to my senses *I* would have been the one he married. He's already admitted that.'

Celena felt as though an icy hand was clutching her heart. She did not doubt Simone's words; Luciano had proved himself to be an expert at evading the truth. She was the one who was the fool—an incredibly gullible fool. She had virtually sat back and let him take over her life.

'But I am prepared to wait,' went on Simone slyly, her cat-like eyes glittering as though a torch had been shone into them. 'It will only be a matter of time before you have served your purpose. Then I will have him all to myself.' These last words were delivered with utter conviction.

Was it Luc or his vast wealth she wanted? contemplated Celena sourly. Did Simone fancy herself as mistress of this house? Had she realised that Luc had more to offer than the man she had left him for?

Suddenly Luc's Mercedes came into sight and stopped her flow of thought, and although resentment and bitterness filled every corner of her mind she could not stem the flood of warmth when she caught sight of him. She had fallen under his spell as absolutely as if he had hypnotised her.

Both girls moved towards the steel-blue car, and as she waited for him to come to her Celena was astonished when Simone pushed herself forward and virtually threw herself into his arms. 'Darling Luciano, I've been waiting for you.'

He looked stunned to see her but did not immediately push the girl away as Celena had expected, and when Simone offered her lips for a kiss he bowed his head low and obliged—and the kiss was long.

Celena could not understand his behaviour. Surely he knew how fragile the thread was that held her to him? If he wanted her to remain his wife throughout his great-grandmother's lifetime then shouldn't he be behaving with more decorum? Or had he missed Simone so much that he could not help himself?

When he turned to Celena his pleasure at seeing her seemed genuine enough, but she caught a glimpse of

Simone's triumph and found that she could not smile in
return.

'I hope you don't mind me coming here,' purred
Simone, watching them both closely. 'But I've missed
you, Luciano. Can I join you for lunch?'

The gall of the girl, thought Celena. Had she no
conscience?

Luc attempted to kiss Celena before he answered but
she ensured that it was brief, pulling away from his
embrace almost before his lips touched hers. He
frowned harshly, obviously wondering what had happened to her in his absence. She had been his to do
with as he'd liked when he'd left yesterday morning;
now she was practically freezing him out.

He turned to Simone and smiled. 'I don't think that
would be a good idea, darling. No one here—er—
knows about you. You should not have come.'

She pouted. 'But I got tired of sitting around waiting.'

Waiting for him to visit her? speculated Celena. How
often had that happened? It was no wonder that he
swore he was not seeing Simone in England; he had her
cosily installed somewhere close at hand. In Enna
probably—or was that too close to home? Wherever,
the thought sickened her. And when Luc took Simone's
elbow and led her a few yards away so that he could
speak to her in private the bitter taste of bile rose in
Celena's throat and threatened to choke her.

'I'm sorry about that,' he said, once Simone had
climbed back into her car. 'I had no idea she would turn
up here.'

'But you did know that she was still in Sicily? You
have been seeing her?' Celena demanded to know.

He lifted his broad shoulders with a nonchalant air.
'Maybe a couple of times.'

'More than that,' she accused. 'Simone told me
herself that you took her to England.'

He looked slightly startled. 'She had business to attend to.'

'So had I,' she snapped, 'but you wouldn't take me. What's the difference?'

'A hell of a lot,' he growled, but he did not say what that difference was.

Celena was furious. 'How long do you plan on keeping her here? Has she spun you some little sob story about this older guy you claim she left you for? Do you believe that she's still in love with you? Is it your massive male ego that prevents you from kicking her out? Or do you still love her? Do you wish you hadn't been so hasty in selecting me for this little charade you've set your mind on?' Her voice rose more shrilly with each question until in the end she was virtually shrieking her words at him.

'That is enough, Celena,' he commanded, his dark eyes narrowed and suddenly angry. 'I do not wish to discuss Simone. Come, let us go inside.'

'You cannot fool me that you don't feel something for her,' she insisted.

'What is that supposed to mean?' he asked coldly.

'I mean the way you kissed her just now, leaving me standing looking like a fool. I know it's only pretence where we're concerned, but heavens, Luc, if you expect me to play the part surely you can too?' Her breast rose and fell as she spoke, her breathing unsteady.

'Maybe *you* should have been the one to throw yourself at me,' he growled impatiently. 'Don't you think you're a little at fault, standing back and letting it happen?'

'I'm not a hussy,' she declared strongly. 'And you didn't have to kiss her so—properly. You looked like lovers.'

They were in the house now and he halted at the door to their sitting room, his lips quirking, his beautiful velvet-brown eyes looking long into hers. 'Are you sure you're not jealous of her, Celena?'

She looked at him coldly. 'Jealousy is one emotion I would never feel where you are concerned.'

His brow flickered, as though he did not quite know what to make of her answer. 'So what has upset you,' he asked, moving into the room and closing the door behind them, 'if it's not Simone?'

'Everything,' she declared emphatically, throwing herself down into one of the deep armchairs. She had not intended airing her grievances this soon, having decided it would be best to charm Luc before asking him to speak to his great-grandmother. But he had caught her off balance and there was no possible way now she could hide her discontent.

'How can that be?' he asked in puzzlement. 'I've only been gone just over twenty-four hours.'

'Long enough for your precious *bisnonna* to upset me,' she proclaimed.

'Bisnonna?' Luc, about to sit down, stood up again and looked at her in shocked disbelief. 'I don't understand. What has she said? What has she done?' His tone suggested that his great-grandmother wasn't capable of upsetting anyone.

Celena closed her eyes for a brief moment and drew in a ragged breath. 'Does being married to you mean that I lose my identity? That I'm not allowed to have a mind of my own? That I cannot do one thing for myself?'

He smiled his relief. 'So that's it—Bisnonna has been interfering. She wants to help you plan things.'

'No, that is not it,' cried Celena, her eyes a stormy grey in her troubled face. 'She doesn't want to help; she simply would not let me go out to the shops by myself. I had to have samples sent here. I couldn't even go and have my hair cut—she sent for her own hairdresser. Dammit, Luc, it's like being in prison.'

When he began to laugh she could not believe her eyes.

'It's not funny,' she expostulated.

'Do you know you're incredibly beautiful when you're angry?'

'Stop trying to distract me,' she thrust furiously. 'I am serious, Luc. I refuse to be treated like this and I want you to tell your great-grandmother. What era does she live in, for heaven's sake?'

He smiled proudly. 'Maybe she does still have her head in the past, but we all look up to her. When my great-grandfather died she was a relatively young woman, but she found a strength that surprised everyone. I appreciate your distress, I know exactly how you feel, but I couldn't possibly tell her what to do. She is the undisputed head of this household.'

And he wanted to take her place! That was the top and bottom of it, thought Celena disappointedly. He could not afford to upset Giacoma because she might very well disinherit him—and this marriage would have been for nothing. 'In that case,' she said, looking at him coldly and disdainfully, 'I have no recourse but to leave. I will not live here and be treated in this manner. It's inhuman of you to expect me to put up with it.'

His smile faded, a severe frown taking its place. 'How many more times do I have to listen to this? Get it into your beautiful head, Celena—you are not going anywhere. I absolutely forbid it.'

Her eyes widened. 'You *forbid* it? How can you? Do you realise that you're as bad as your great-grandmother? You cannot keep me here against my will, Luciano; you cannot place all these restrictions on me. I don't believe that I would be in any danger going out on my own; I think you're being singularly bloody-minded for the simple reason that if I walk out you'll be left with egg on your face.'

She had expected further anger; instead a slow, humourless smile spread across his features. 'If that is truly what you think then maybe I shall have to make sure that you don't want to leave.' He came purposefully towards her.

Celena pushed herself hurriedly to her feet but it was an unwise move because she somehow found herself in his arms, held hard against a savagely masculine body that, despite her fury, had the power to arouse every single one of her base instincts.

She fought to free herself but in vain. 'Let me go, you brute,' she cried, straining against him. 'You cannot do this.'

A wicked grin split his face. 'I can do what I like, Celena,' he muttered, his lips grazing hers. It was the lightest touch and yet it sent shuddering sensations through her veins.

The tip of his tongue touched her lips next, tracing their outline—slow, sensual, sensitive movements that triggered desire through the very heart of her. Without realising what she was doing Celena urged her body feverishly towards his. It was inevitable; he only had to touch her for her to melt. She had been a fool to let him anywhere near her.

'My Celena,' he muttered possessively, his lips still over hers. And his hand moved to cup her breast through the thin voile of her dress.

She drew in a sharp breath of arousal. It was so beautiful, so incredibly exciting. How could he do this to her so quickly? Why was she so weak? Because you love him, answered a little voice inside her head. And the fact that he did not love her made no difference at all.

When his other hand drew down the zip on the back

of her dress she wanted to demur but couldn't. All sane
reasoning had fled. The soft material was pushed gently
from her shoulders, incredibly gently, each movement
an erotic stroke. Her white satin bra was disposed of
next, her breasts revealed to his hungry eyes in all their
naked, blazing glory, pink tips erect, almost begging to
be touched.

He pushed her gently down onto a soft leather sofa
and then knelt in front of her, and it was not his hands
that assaulted her breasts but his mouth. He had done
it before, many times in the last week, but for some
reason her enjoyment now was greater. Her heart
thundered and she felt she wanted to die from the
sheer, exquisite rapture of his tongue ravaging this most
sensitive part of her.

His teeth gnawed and bit—quite hard—but it was a
pleasurable hurt and she held his head against her,
revelling in the feel of its strong shape, entwining her
fingers through the rich thickness of his hair.

'Oh, Celena, what you do to me,' he muttered thickly
at length, lifting glazed eyes to her face.

And he to her! And yet somehow she found the
strength to voice a faint protest. 'I know why you're
doing this, Luc, and it's not going to work. I won't
be—'

She was effectively silenced by his mouth, warm and
moist, tasting of her own perfumed skin, and she was
lost—her lips devouring his hungrily, giving away her
inner torment, letting him see that he had the power to
take over her body whenever he wished, that it was a
weapon in his favour and whenever he used it he would
get his own way. She hated herself for it but there was
nothing she could do.

His mouth left hers to burn a trail down her throat,
his tongue lingering for a moment on the fluttering
pulse at its base, devouring again the aching fullness

of her breasts before searing the flatness of her stomach. When his fingers eased inside the white satin of her panties she was beyond rational thought and arched her body instinctively.

At that precise instant the door to their private sitting room burst open.

CHAPTER TEN

'LUCIANO, I saw you come back. I just wanted to tell you that—'

Luc's sister's face was a picture of embarrassment when she saw Celena lying naked on the couch with Luc bent over her. 'I'm sorry; I do apologise,' she mumbled, her face suffusing with colour, and she closed the door again quickly. They could hear her footsteps hastening away.

If Luc was disconcerted too it did not show, thought Celena; he still had the same hungry expression.

'Maybe we should make a habit of locking the door,' he growled good-humouredly, but when he showed every intention of resuming where they had left off she hastily shook her head, snatching up her dress as she pushed herself to her feet. 'I think I ought to thank Gabriella for bringing me to my senses. You're very clever, Luc; I nearly submitted.'

A deep frown carved his brow. 'There was nothing clever about it, Celena; it's a case of mutual attraction drawing us together—there is nothing either of us can do to stop it.'

He was right, of course, but she looked at him coldly and distantly as she stepped into the dress, hiding every vestige of desire that still remained inside her. 'Are you denying that it was a deliberate attempt to stop me from leaving?'

To her surprise he shook his head. 'I freely admit that was my intention, but it was also a case of proving to you that you'd be losing a hell of a lot if you did return to England. Don't you agree, Celena, that your

140

life would be an empty shell, that staying here would be a whole lot more—satisfying?'

'Sex isn't everything,' she snapped, struggling with the zip, going suddenly still when he took over the task, his fingers against her skin recreating the sensations that had mounted within her only a few minutes ago.

'I thought it was something more,' he said softly, his voice disturbingly close to her ear. 'I thought we had reached a different level.' His hands were on her shoulders, gently massaging, urging her back against him. 'These last few days you've—'

'You're surely not of the opinion that I'm beginning to fall in love with you?' she queried, jerking away from him, putting all the heat of her emotions into those words, making it sound as though the very thought was anathema to her. He must never know; if he had the slightest suspicion of how she felt, how she truly felt deep down inside, he would lose no opportunity in using it to his advantage.

A muscle jerked in his jaw but his voice was admirably under control. 'Not love—I don't expect that—but I did feel that we had an understanding.'

'Absolutely,' she retorted, feeling better now that there was space between them. 'This is a job—a job with a difference, I admit—and there are parts of it that. . .I quite enjoy—I admit that also—but that's as far as it goes. And because it's a job I can quit any time I like.' Her voice was stronger now and absolutely determined. 'I will not let you use emotional blackmail; emotions don't enter into it.'

'So you're going to leave, whatever I say?' His velvet-brown eyes, so wonderfully soft at times, were like obsidian.

'If I don't get my freedom, yes,' she answered, chin high. 'I won't be kept a prisoner here, Luc. I want to be free to go shopping or walking by myself. Surely that's not too much to ask?'

'I appreciate what you're saying,' he said, 'but I think you do not fully understand what sort of a family you are married into.' He stood tall, looking down at her with that imperious way he had, but she was not daunted.

'It wasn't my choice,' she flung at him. 'I refuse to conform. And if you're going to run this household the way your great-grandmother does then God help everybody. I shall be glad to be out of it.'

His eyes narrowed. 'I shall run it as I think fit, and in the meantime I would not dream of asking Bisnonna for any dispensation on your behalf.'

'But she must know that I come from a totally different background,' Celena protested. 'She cannot take my freedom away from me, and nor can you.'

His face was mask-like. 'There are lots of things you do not understand, but in any case it would be incorrect for a new member of the family to try and alter things.'

Celena's eyes flashed coldly. 'I am not a member of your family—not in the true sense of the word.'

'But no one knows that, do they?' There was a cruel twist to his lips now, his face all hard, uncompromising angles. 'And it's not as though it's for ever. I think you're being a touch unreasonable.'

'Unreasonable?' she echoed. 'You don't truly appreciate what I'm going through, Luc. I have led an independent life for years; I don't like such restrictions being placed on me. Would Simone have meekly complied? I somehow don't think so.'

'Let's leave Simone out of this,' he rasped.

Because he knew she was right! she thought. 'Why didn't you tell me what your great-grandmother was like before you brought me out here?' she asked fiercely, and then added, 'No, don't answer; I was conned right from the beginning, wasn't I? "I want you to work on the most important undertaking of my life," you said. "You are the very person I have been looking for. You have exactly the right qualifications." I should have known straight away that you weren't talking about a normal job. Did you really think I'd meekly and willingly fit in with the role you had planned for me?'

His brows rose. 'I thought there was a strong possibility that you would "fit in", as you so drolly put it, otherwise I wouldn't have considered asking you.'

'Or perhaps you thought that the size of the salary you offered would ensure I co-operated?' Celena kept her tone deliberately hard even though her body still felt a wickedly traitorous response.

He lifted his shoulders. 'You have to admit it is more than generous—and is still going into your account every month.'

'And some good it's doing me there,' she riposted. 'You've taken my passport; you've taken my credit cards; my money's in my bank account in England. Despite my asking you to open me a new one here you haven't.' And it was clear why—he had no intention of letting her go until she had served her purpose, until he was the undisputed head of the Segurini dynasty. 'What the hell am I supposed to do?'

He and his great-grandmother were two of a pair with their rigid, unbreakable rules. If this was aristocracy then give her the common person every time, she thought. Was it really too much to ask that she be given some freedom?

He gave a twisted smile. 'I had hoped you would be happy here.'

'I could be, without the restrictions,' she admitted, and amazed even herself by saying so.

Luc grimaced. 'It is simply unfortunate that I had to go back to England so soon.'

'If you'd taken me with you there would have been no problem,' she pointed out. 'And why do we have to live here? Why can't we have a house of our own?' Perhaps then she would be free to come and go as she pleased.

'Because,' he told her tetchily, 'one day this will be mine. I see no point in buying another place that we would have to sell when. . .'

His voice tailed off but Celena knew that he meant when his great-grandmother finally died. There had been almost a touch of poignancy in his tone, as though he really did care, as though he did not want that to happen for a long time yet. But she knew that this could not be true, that material things meant so much more to him, and she shook her head. 'So, if I stay, I have to put up with these impossible limitations?'

'I'm hoping not to go away again, Celena,' he told her. 'It's become clear to me that I can't let go the reins as quickly and as smoothly as I had hoped, so what I plan to do is install an office here in order that I can keep in close touch with London.'

'You do?' Celena smiled widely all of a sudden, glad that he was of the same opinion as herself. 'And I'd be able to help you? I'd be able to work again? We could concentrate on the accounts here in Sicily?'

He smiled at her enthusiasm. 'I hadn't realised how career-minded you are.'

'I much prefer it to running a house,' she told him firmly.

'Then perhaps we can work something out. Why don't we find Francesca and see if she can find us something for lunch?'

Celena realised to her dismay that she had given in and wondered for a moment whether she had done the

right thing—not that she had had very much choice—
she was trapped whether she liked it or not.

Her bitter resentment over the restrictions being
placed on her, over the way her life was no longer her
own, over the way Luc thought she ought to comply
without complaint since he was paying her a healthy
salary was growing daily—and one day, she felt sure, it
would kill the love she felt for him.

Since moving into their own suite of rooms Celena
had done all their cooking, but for once it suited her to
let Francesca feed them; she felt a need to get out of
the confines of their apartment, where there was every
danger that Luc would want to make love again. It was
his answer to everything; he knew she would always
succumb and that whatever had been bothering her
would fade into the background of her mind.

After they had eaten she asked if they could go for a
drive. 'If I don't get out of this house I shall go mad,'
she told him.

But he shook his head. 'I'm afraid that's not possible,
Celena. I have many phone calls to make; I want to get
things moving straight away.'

'Then perhaps I can help you,' she suggested
hopefully.

'I think not at this stage,' he said, and already his
mind was on other things. 'Surely you still have lots to
do?'

Like choosing wallpaper and curtain fabrics! And
when she had got it all to her own taste she would be
sent back to England! Was it any wonder she had no
interest? 'I think you ought to employ an interior
designer,' she told him curtly.

Luc frowned, distracted momentarily, surprised by
her suggestion. 'If that is what you wish. I thought you
would enjoy it; I thought it would keep you happily
occupied.'

'Well, it doesn't,' she snapped. 'I don't see the point when I won't be here for ever.'

His eyes narrowed and Celena saw a flicker of something that she could not understand. 'Very well,' he said tersely.

They parted company and Celena went out into the garden while he shut himself away in his study. She was fuming, both because he refused to lift the restrictions he had placed on her and because he wouldn't let her help him now. The situation was getting worse instead of better and the unfortunate thing was that she could do nothing about it.

Even the beautiful ivy-leafed geranium, trailing its profusion of pink over the stone walls, and the bright scarlet of the pomegranate flowers failed to cheer her and in the end she decided defiantly to take a walk into Enna. Luc and his great-grandmother could say what they liked; this confinement was driving her mad.

The brisk walk and the fresh air did her good and she found the ancient alleyways enchanting and the busy piazzas comforting. She had not intended to stop by Raimondo Vittorini's bar, but he caught sight of her as she strolled past, and called out her name.

She paused and he came up to her and his smile of pleasure at seeing her again was infectious. 'Celena, I have wondered how you are—and your new husband too, of course. I hear many things about what a beautiful bride you were.'

Celena smiled self-consciously. 'It was quite an occasion.'

'It overwhelmed you?'

Surprised at how intuitive he was, she nodded.

'And where is your husband now? Surely he is not in England again?'

'No, no,' she answered quickly. 'He was just too busy to come.'

'I see,' he said, but it was clear he didn't. 'Would you have time to take a glass of wine with me?'

I have all the time in the world, answered Celena silently, but she knew it would be the wrong thing to do. If someone saw them, if Luc found out, there would be hell to pay. So she shook her head. 'I'm afraid not; I'm just heading back now.'

He spread his hands. 'Maybe some other time.'

'Maybe,' she agreed.

Back at the big house Luc had not even missed her; he did not emerge from his study until over an hour later. Celena was curled up in a corner of the sofa with a magazine.

She looked up when he entered, felt her pulses leaping in response to his raw masculinity—this was something that would, unfortunately, never go away—but her smile was less than welcoming. 'Is it all done?'

He stretched and yawned. 'I think so. Some of the stuff will arrive tomorrow, the computer system will take a little longer, but within a couple of weeks we should be up and running. I'm starving; what have we got for supper?'

Food had been the last thing on Celena's mind and she shrugged. 'Nothing.'

He frowned. 'You've not prepared a meal?'

She shook her head.

'Then what have you been doing?'

'This and that,' she said with a nonchalant shrug. 'Not very much.'

'So why haven't you cooked?'

'Because I didn't know what time you'd be finished,' she retorted.

He looked at her long and hard. 'I do not understand you, Celena. Most women would give their eye-teeth to be in your position—no money worries, a hairdresser

POWERFUL PERSUASION

148

and dressmaker on call. Is cooking a simple meal too much for you under those circumstances?'

'I am not most people,' she retorted. 'You chose unwisely, Luc.'

'I think not,' he said. 'I think it is taking you time to adjust, that is all. Go and get changed; we'll eat out.'

'I'm not hungry,' she told him.

A frown made jagged lines across his brow. 'You were complaining earlier about never going anywhere.'

Celena shrugged. 'Maybe I was, but now I don't feel like it.'

Her attitude angered him and he rasped, 'Well, I do, and you are coming whether you like it or not.' His eyes blazed into hers. 'Stop behaving like a spoilt child, Celena, and act like the woman you are.'

Reluctantly she got to her feet, and he followed her up to their bedroom. He watched her as she undressed, eyes hooded and unreadable; he watched as she padded across to the bathroom, stampeding her pulses even though she did her best to ignore him, and when she switched on the shower and stepped beneath the hot jets—he was stripped naked and right behind her.

Celena had no time to object; the glass door closed and their bodies came together—his lean and hard and filled with controlled passion, hers soft and gently rounded and already beginning to tremble.

When she'd agreed to marry Luc she had not anticipated that he would make such demands on her. A marriage of convenience, a job, she had thought, never expecting that he would want to fulfil his roll to the nth degree.

And yet, despite knowing that it was no more than a physical attraction on his part, she could not summon up the strength to resist him. The pleasure was magical, as though a part of her merged into him every time they made love. Soon, if she wasn't careful, he would own her completely and she would never be able to leave.

His hands soaped her body, slowly, tantalisingly, every inch of her, every secret part, and she stood there with closed eyes, her breathing growing laboured, feeling that if it went on for much longer she would melt altogether and disappear down the plughole.

When he had aroused every inch of her, when there was not one part of her that he had not touched, that he had not excited beyond description, he silently put the soap into her hand and without being bidden Celena did the same to him.

It was unbearably erotic, running her hands over the silken hardness of his body, over his complete male arousal, and long before she had finished Celena ached for him to make love to her, right here and now with the hot jets of water raining down on them, with her heart thudding fit to burst.

And as if he had read her mind he suddenly pulled her against him, urgently and hungrily, his fingers strong and fierce on her back, his body hot. And it was like the first time he had ever made love to her—intense and powerful and over far too quickly.

They continued to hold each other and the water still washed over them but neither noticed. They were both filled with the magical aftermath of euphoria, needing to maintain physical contact, to feel the bonding that was so perfect, so right—and so important, as far as Celena was concerned.

'My beautiful, heady, sweet Celena,' he muttered thickly and desperately, after what seemed like aeons of standing locked together, and she had no qualms about letting him make love to her a second time. The whole happening went far beyond anything she had ever imagined; it was an experience to surpass all experiences—and when their marriage ended she would still have these wonderful, wonderful memories.

They truly defied description, transcending all earthly feelings, and she deeply regretted that theirs wasn't a true loving relationship. It seemed such a pity that what they had found together couldn't be theirs for ever.

On the other hand, loving a man the way she loved Luc was excruciatingly painful and in one respect it would have been better if they didn't have these moments of tenderness, if he was arrogant and domineering and totally unbearable at all times—then her love would die and when the time came for her to go she wouldn't be hurt.

She wondered what thoughts were going through Luc's mind. Or was the experience no different from that with any other girl? Was it, perhaps, even better with others? With Simone, for instance? It was a sobering thought, especially when she remembered that he had been seeing her recently, but Celena determinedly pushed it to the back of her mind. For the moment she wanted nothing to spoil this magical interlude.

Afterwards he towelled her dry, and this big man was so gentle, so careful, so devoted to what he was doing that Celena found it difficult to believe that he did not love her too. It was amazing how her feelings had changed when less than half an hour ago she had been frantic to escape.

Luc touched her lips with his fingertips. 'I'm glad you're happy again, Celena.'

'How can I help it when you're such a fantastic lover?' she asked softly, and surprised even herself by her answer.

His eyes narrowed. 'Is that important to you?'

She shrugged and tried to appear nonchalant. 'I

wouldn't be able to go through with the charade otherwise.'

'Let's get dressed,' he said roughly. 'Will you wear your ivory dress for me?'

The one with all the buttons! Was it because he wanted to prolong these moments of intimacy? wondered Celena, feeling a further surge of warm, joyous emotion. Because he too felt a oneness that was unique? Or was it all wishful thinking on her part?

She fetched the dress from the wardrobe and slid into it, savouring the sensual feel of the silk against her skin. And when Luc did it up for her it was as though she was being made love to all over again.

It was almost a pity that they were going out, she thought. It would have been good to stop in with him now, to continue the evening in the same vein. Nevertheless she looked forward to spending the next few hours in his company and felt a painful stab of disappointment when they walked into the restaurant a short time later and the first person she saw was Simone.

'What is *she* doing here?' Celena muttered, pulling away from Luc's arm, which was proprietorially around her waist.

'I have no idea,' he admitted quietly, giving Celena no indication of whether he was pleased to see his exgirlfriend or otherwise, or whether he was even surprised to see her.

Simone, however, was quite clearly overjoyed to see Luc and gave him a brilliant smile, beckoning him over to join her and her companion, who, Celena noted with a jolt of unease, when she finally managed to drag her eyes away from the girl, was no other than Raimondo Vittorini. What on earth were they doing together?

Raimondo smiled warmly at Celena and she heard alarm bells ring in her head and knew that she dared not respond. To her relief Luc declined Simone's invitation, and with a quiet word in the waiter's ear they were led to a table in a discreet corner well away from the other couple, but not before Celena had been directed a coldly hostile glare from the girl who looked so much like her.

'I'm sorry about this,' Luc said, having made sure that Celena sat with her back to the others. Not that it made her feel any better; she was still highly conscious of Simone's animosity.

'You mean you're sorry that Simone's not the one you're out with?' asked Celena caustically.

His lips twisted, seeming unconcerned by her anger. 'When are you going to accept that it is over between us?'

'Not until she's well and truly back in England,' Celena snapped. 'You must be giving her some encouragement, otherwise why would she stay?'

He shrugged. 'She has, perhaps unfortunately, taken a liking to my country.'

'And I'm supposed to believe that it is Sicily she is in love with and not you?' she asked coldly. 'Have you eaten here with her?' It was an expensive-looking place in the mountains, with low lighting and an atmosphere certainly conducive to romance. Celena was consumed with bitter jealousy.

His lips quirked. 'Would it bother you if I had?'

Celena suddenly did not want to know. 'Forget it,' she said tartly. 'I have no right to ask such a question.' And she took a menu from the hovering waiter.

'As my wife you have every right,' he said, much to her surprise.

Celena allowed her eyes to widen. 'You're talking as though I'm a *proper* wife. That will never be the case, Luc.' And she deliberately made her tone hard.

She bent her head over the menu and when she looked at him again he was studying his also. It broke

her heart to have to speak to him like this but she felt
it was imperative on occasions to put a certain distance
between them, otherwise she would, without a doubt,
give away her true feelings.

'Have you decided?' He looked up and caught her
watching him and Celena's heart missed a beat. He was
devastatingly handsome—and such a fantastic lover—
and despite everything, if the truth were known, she
wanted him for ever.

She nodded. 'I thought for antipasto I'd have the
sarde a beccafico, followed by *impanata di pescespada*.'

'An excellent choice,' he agreed. 'I'll have the swordfish too, but to begin with I think the asparagus
omelette.'

Their choices made, Celena had no menu to hide
behind, but she would have been perfectly content had
Simone not been in the same room. As it was, she felt
uncomfortable and could not help wondering whether
the other girl's eyes were more on Luciano than her
companion.

'I didn't know that Simone was friends with
Raimondo,' she said. It puzzled her, seeing the two of
them together.

Luc's eyes narrowed. 'Does it bother you?' he rasped.

Celena looked at him sharply. 'Of course not.
Raimondo is very charming, but I'm not interested in
him—not in the way you seem to be suggesting.'

Luc looked doubtful. 'His eyes certainly lit up when
you entered the room.'

Celena had seen only Simone in those first few
seconds so had no idea whether Luc was speaking the
truth. 'I'm quite sure you're imagining things.'

'I don't think so,' he answered coolly. 'Even now his
eyes are on you.'

'As yours are on Simone,' she snapped. 'Don't try
and make me feel guilty, Luc.'

The whole meal remained strained as far as Celena was concerned. Although she enjoyed her stuffed sardines, and the swordfish pie with its delicate crust flavoured with orange was delicious, she was too aware of the other girl's interest in Luc to really relax, which was a shame, considering the pleasure they had found in each other's bodies earlier.

She felt bitterly resentful that Simone should ruin things twice in one day, and when the two of them came up to their table as soon as they had finished eating and Simone said, 'Can we join you for drinks?' Celena felt like spitting in her eye. She willed Luc to refuse.

Instead, as she had known he would, he smiled—the sort of smile that melted a girl's heart whether she was in love with him or not. 'Of course,' he said. 'You're very welcome.'

CHAPTER ELEVEN

'I BELIEVE you and Raimondo have already met,' Simone said to Celena as Luc signalled to the waiter to bring two extra chairs.

'Yes,' agreed Celena, acknowledging Raimondo, being careful not to put too much warmth into her smile, knowing that her husband would deliberately misinterpret it if she did.

'Wasn't it this very afternoon that you last saw each other?' asked the other girl slyly.

Celena gave an inward groan as she felt Luc's eyes target her, but there was no point in lying. 'As a matter of fact, yes,' she answered, not looking at her husband, keeping her eyes on Simone instead.

The girl who was uncannily like her looked as though she was thoroughly enjoying herself. 'Raimondo actually mistook me for you; that is how *we* met. I was totally confused at first when this strange man took me into his arms and kissed me.'

Luciano's expression became thunderous.

Celena curled her hands into fists beneath the table.

Raimondo said quickly, 'Simone, you are exaggerating; I did nothing of the—'

'Don't be embarrassed, Raimondo,' she cut in, laughing. 'I really rather liked it.'

'Please, do not believe everything this girl says,' said Raimondo to Luc. 'It is correct, I did mistake her for Celena, but I most certainly did not—'

'I think I have heard enough,' interrupted Luciano damningly, and Celena grew ice-cold. Luc would be too polite to cause a scene now but as soon as they were alone the sparks would most definitely fly.

For the next few minutes Simone paid more attention to Luc than her companion, leaving Raimondo no choice but to talk to Celena. They very carefully kept their topic of conversation impersonal, but Celena knew that Luc was listening even though he seemed to be giving Simone his full attention. And the girl was certainly devoting herself to him, taking no pains at all to hide her feelings. It was embarrassing to see.

There was no doubt in Celena's mind that Simone had engineered her meeting with Raimondo. The other girl had no doubt spotted her talking to him on·that first occasion, and it would have been Simone who'd told Luc. And it was probably Simone's suggestion that they dine in this particular restaurant, perhaps knowing that it was one of Luc's favourite eating places.

As she sipped the last of her brandy Celena glanced at Luc out of the corner of her eye and saw that he was watching her.

'If you're ready we'll go,' he said, and his smile, to all outward appearances, was warm. But Celena sensed the fury in his heart and knew that she wasn't in for an easy time, that the interrogation about to take place would probably leave her devastated.

'Do you have to leave so soon?' asked Simone, her hand resting on Luc's arm, her green eyes wide and plaintive, her voice pleading.

'I'm afraid so,' he told her softly. 'Celena and I plan on an early night.'

Simone frowned, obviously getting the wrong idea, wondering how he could say such a thing when she had told him very plainly that his wife had been seeing another man behind his back. And she cast a malevolent glance in Celena's direction, almost as though she was accusing her of making the suggestion.

Celena ignored her and pushed her chair back, saying a careful goodbye to Raimondo. Luc rose also, shook Raimondo's hand, albeit reluctantly, kissed Simone warmly and lingeringly, then put his arm around Celena's waist as they left the restaurant.

Immediately they were out of sight, however, his arm fell to his side. 'Explain yourself, Celena,' he said coldly.

'There is nothing to explain,' she said, looking at him calmly.

'I happen to think there is,' he rasped.

'I went for a walk, that is all,' she told him, refusing to let herself get worked up.

'Without telling me?'

'You were busy,' she insisted, 'and I was fed up, absolutely bored out of my mind. I am not going to be kept prisoner, Luc—you can say what you like.'

They stopped at the car but he did not open the door. He stood with his back to it, his eyes fiercely accusing. 'Are you sure it wasn't a secret tryst?'

Her eyes suddenly blazed. 'You have a disgusting mind, Luc.'

'I saw Raimondo's eyes on you.'

'And I saw yours on Simone,' she retorted. 'Don't try to tell me what to do when it's obvious that your little romance is not over. I've had some very meaningful conversations with Simone; I know exactly what the position is.'

Dark brows rose. 'Hasn't it occurred to you that Simone could be exaggerating? The lady wants me back; I'm fully aware of that.'

'And you're doing nothing to discourage her,' snapped Celena. 'In fact you have the best of both worlds—the girl you love, and the girl you married for—what shall I say?—personal reasons. Perhaps you wish you hadn't been so hasty now that Simone's back on the scene? I've no doubt she'd have made a better wife than me.'

He ignored her question, retaliating with one of his own. 'I suppose it's because of Simone that you thought you'd have a little fun with Raimondo, is that it?' he demanded harshly.

Celena shook her head, her lips as tight as his, her eyes blazing. 'I had no intention of speaking to Raimondo when I went out today, but he saw me and it would have been impolite to ignore him. He's a nice guy, I like him, but that's as far as it goes. I cannot see why you object to me speaking to him. He has no idea that our marriage is anything other than normal; at least, he didn't until today. I'm not sure what he thinks after Simone's little exhibition.'

Luc's eyes were like shards of ice. 'If you know what's good for you you won't go out alone again. Had I known how desperate you were I would have come with you.'

'Really?' she jeered. 'Are you forgetting I suggested it but you were too busy? I'm beginning to wonder whether it will be a good thing, your working from home. Something tells me you'll still never have time for me.' Her eyes sparked her hostility. 'I know this isn't a proper marriage but you could at least consider *my* feelings.'

He suddenly yanked open the car door, allowing her to slide inside. 'And you could consider mine,' he retorted tersely and coldly, getting in himself. Slamming the car into gear, he roared out of the car park. 'I absolutely forbid you to speak to Raimondo again. No wife of a Segurini looks at another man; no one would dare to bring shame and humiliation to the family name.'

Celena gasped and looked at him coldly and haughtily. 'Anyone would think I'd been to bed with him. What would you like to do, put a chastity belt on me?'

'Don't mock, Celena,' he rasped. 'I am perfectly serious.'

'Serious?' she questioned. 'You're deranged. And I must have been out of my mind in agreeing to marry you. It's a farce; it's a ridiculous state of affairs.'

'It could be so different,' he muttered, his tone low all of a sudden.

'Easily,' she snapped, '*if* we were in love with each other; but as there is no possibility of that then you'll have to put up with me as I am—or not at all. If I can't be trusted to behave with integrity, without all these warnings from you, then I think you're best well rid of me.'

'*Maledizione!*' he swore. 'All these threats to leave when you know very well that you cannot.'

They were racing down the twisting mountain road and Celena began to fear for her safety. 'Don't you think you ought to slow down?'

'I know what I'm doing,' he growled.

She closed her eyes and clung to the edge of her seat and after a few moments she felt their headlong pace slacken. When she finally looked up Luc's hands were more relaxed on the wheel, though when she dared glance at his face his features were still taut.

When they arrived back at the *palazzo* Celena breathed more easily, scrambling out of the car and walking briskly towards the house without waiting for Luc.

Maybe, with a bit of luck, he would stay downstairs and pour himself a nightcap, while she could slip into bed and, hopefully, be asleep before he came up. And, to begin with, her plan began to work. Luc did not follow her; she heard him go into his study, knowing it was that room he entered because the hinges creaked in a particular way.

It was not until she was in their bedroom that she remembered which dress she was wearing. It meant either going to bed in it—which would be criminal with such an expensive and beautiful garment—or going down again and asking Luc to unbutton it for her!

Recalling where it had led the last time, Celena was reluctant to do this—but what alternative had she? Her question was answered when Luc entered the room. His smile was grim, revealing all too clearly that he had not got over his ill humour. 'I thought you might need a hand.'

'I'm sorry if it inconveniences you,' she said tightly. 'I think it would be best if I did not wear this dress again; it causes too much trouble.'

'It's no trouble,' he answered gruffly, approaching the task in a very businesslike manner, undoing the buttons in no time at all, making Celena realise that he had been playing a very definite game on the previous occasion. He did not even let the dress fall from her shoulders before leaving the room again. Celena felt very close to tears; he could not have made his feelings more clear.

Although she was still wide awake when Luc eventually came to bed Celena pretended to be asleep, and he lay with his back to her, careful not to touch her, and the tears she had held back so long slid silently down her cheeks.

She dreamt that she was walking along the top of a very narrow and very icy mountain ridge when suddenly she lost her footing and began tumbling down the mountainside. Luc appeared from nowhere and saved her, lifting her in arms that were as strong as steel. 'You are safe with me,' he murmured, 'my beautiful, beautiful Celena. I love you and I adore you and I must have you—here and now.' With an urgency that was as exciting as it was surprising he began to tear off her clothes.

Celena did not resist, could not resist, and when she was naked, not feeling the icy-cold air that blew around them, she linked her arms around his neck and cried passionately, 'Oh, my darling, I love you too, and I want you so desperately.'

It was a magical experience, out there in the icy air— but as soon as Luc had satisfied himself he grew into a giant and plucked her from the ground between thumb and forefinger and threw her high into the air.

She felt herself twisting and turning, over and over, higher and higher, coming almost to a standstill before she began to fall, plummeting suddenly with tremendous speed. The mountain got closer and larger and just as she was about to smash into it, as her blood-curdling screams rent the air she woke up.

It was daylight and Luc was standing over her, and all she could see was the great giant bulk of him. She began to scream again. 'Get away from me,' she cried. 'Get away!'

'Who would you prefer—Raimondo?' he asked icily.

By this time Celena was properly awake and she sat up and looked at him with surprised eyes. 'What the hell is that supposed to mean?'

'You were dreaming about him, that's what you were doing,' he rasped. 'You told him you loved him; you begged him to make love to you. What I would like to know is what is really going on between you?'

'You're wrong,' cried Celena. 'It wasn't Raimondo, it was you I was dreaming about—and I certainly didn't mean it when I said I loved you.' Her lip curled contemptuously. He had used her and thrown her away in her dream just as he was doing in real life. 'I hate you, Luc, I hate you, and if things get too unbearable I shall find a way of leaving, make no mistake about that.'

Their eyes met and warred and the air was thick with tension—and electricity! Even in the midst of her anger Celena could not deny the spark that still ran from him to her; it was, if possible, even more intense. She wished she had some control over it; she wished her love for Luc wouldn't keep rearing its head and clouding her vision.

She was the first to look away, then was taken completely by surprise when Luc's hands clamped on her face, turning it up to his, his mouth imprisoning hers in a kiss that was both devastating and punishing. It lasted for no more than a few seconds and yet it drained every ounce of energy from her.

'One of many constant reminders you will get that you belong to me—and only me.' The threatening growl came from deep in his throat and his eyes were menacingly dark upon hers. Then he turned abruptly and left the room.

Celena shuddered and sprang out of bed, heading for the bathroom and a much needed shower. They were pointless words—if he only knew it. She had no feelings for Raimondo whatsoever.

It was her dream that troubled her. It had been very profound, perfectly mirroring her circumstances. Did it really mean that Luc would discard her so brutally at the end of it all? She hated the thought; her life would be so empty after Luc.

After towelling herself dry and pulling on a cotton skirt and blouse Celena made her way downstairs. She had no idea what sort of day lay ahead; it had certainly not got off to a very good start.

Luc wasn't in the kitchen; she found him in his study. 'Don't you want any breakfast?' she asked.

He looked at her coldly. 'If you can force yourself to cook for me, yes.'

Celena frowned. 'It's not only the dream, is it? You're still angry because I dared to go for a walk yesterday afternoon, and I dared to speak to another man. It doesn't matter that you can do whatever you like with Simone.' Her eyes challenged his. 'It's all one-sided, isn't it, this arrangement?'

He sprang suddenly to his feet and took her by the shoulders. 'I am hurt, Celena, that you did not even tell me that you had been out. However, contrary to what you might think, I have no wish to continue this argument; I think I've made my point. After breakfast you can help me set up the office.'

Celena eyed him stonily, glad that he was giving her something positive to do but not altogether sure it would work. The atmosphere between them at this moment was not exactly conducive to a good working relationship.

She left him there while she fixed their breakfast. Luc liked bacon and eggs whereas she was content with jam croissants. They both preferred coffee to tea—except Earl Grey on occasions—and when the meal was ready she gave him a call.

When he did not answer she went along to his study, thinking that perhaps he had not heard. The door was ajar and he was on the telephone. Not meaning to listen, Celena paused when she heard him say, 'Simone, I'm afraid that is impossible today.' His voice was low and intimate and she turned and fled. For him to be speaking to this other girl so early in the morning, especially after seeing her last night, could mean only one thing.

When he eventually appeared his breakfast was congealing on the plate and Celena, having finished both her croissant and her coffee, was about to leave the table.

He looked sharply at her and then at the plate. 'What is this?'

'Didn't you hear me call to say that it was ready?' she asked with professed innocence.

'I was on the telephone.'

'Oh, really? What was so important that you let your breakfast get cold?'

'As a matter of fact I was talking to Simone.'

Celena was surprised by the admission.

'She wondered whether she could help; I told her last night that I was setting up an office here.'

'And what did you say?' He needn't think that she would work alongside the other girl. If Simone came she was definitely out.

'That it wasn't necessary, that you were helping and your knowledge of the company would be of more advantage. She has never done office work before; she would be more a hindrance than a help.'

'Then why do you think she offered?'

'Most likely because she has nothing else to do.'

Or because she wanted to be with him! 'If you would prefer Simone then I—'

'I want you, Celena, or no one,' he cut in abruptly.

'I'll cook you some more bacon,' she said, feeling a small measure of triumph.

'Don't bother; I'll have croissants,' he answered, helping himself from the basket.

Although Celena was pleased that he had turned down Simone's offer she could not help recalling the warmth in his voice as he'd spoken to her. He could deny all he liked that there was nothing between them; the facts proved otherwise.

After breakfast they both went along to the room he was going to use as his new office, calling on Francesca's father to help move furniture, organising it so that there was room for the new desks and filing cabinets due that morning, as well as the computer equipment coming later in the week.

Celena quite enjoyed working alongside Luc, and in his business mode he forgot their differences. Not that he was loving—far from it. He barked out orders and issued instructions and she was expected to execute them immediately.

Later in the day a new telephone was installed and a fax machine and Celena could not help wondering what Luc's great-grandmother would make of it. 'Have you told Giacoma?' she asked, voicing her thoughts out loud.

'Told her what?' he asked with a swift frown.

'About all of this.'

He grinned suddenly. 'Not yet.'

'I bet she's seen all the comings and goings. Will she object, do you think?'

'Not if it's going to keep me here,' he said confidently, making Celena realise that Luc could get away with murder as far as his great-grandmother was concerned.

'She loves you dearly, doesn't she?'

'As I do her,' he agreed.

The sincerity in his tone made it difficult for Celena to accept that he was lying. And yet she had heard from two separate sources that his inheritance was of paramount importance to him. It had to be the truth.

During the next few days Celena hardly had time to think, but then, all of a sudden, everything was in place. Luc kept in constant touch with London either by fax or telephone. He spent hours at a time in front of the computer, studying facts and figures, but because, as yet, he was generating no new business here in Sicily there was nothing for Celena to do.

In fact if she turned up in his office he made it very clear that she was in the way, and although she tried to generate some enthusiasm for refurbishing their apartment she found that impossible too, and in the end outside contractors were brought in.

She grew more and more discontented. 'Can I borrow your car?' she asked Luc one day, without much hope of having her request granted. 'I thought I'd drive into Palermo.'

'Why do you want to go there?' he asked, with ill-concealed impatience at the interruption.

'Because if I don't do something I'll go out of my mind,' she retorted. 'I thought when you opened your office that you'd find me work, not ignore me—after all, I am your employee,' she finished, her tone cold.

'You're more than that,' he pointed out gruffly.

Her brows slid up. 'Am I?'

'You're my wife.'

'When it suits you.' Her tone was condemning. 'Most of the time you're hardly aware of my presence.'

'That is not right, Celena.' His brown eyes were suddenly intent upon hers. 'You are never very far from my thoughts.'

Her brows lifted; she was not sure that she believed him. 'Then why do you shut me out?'

'My work has always come first.'

'In other words you're not used to having a wife around. You forget that she would like some of your time too.'

'Most wives seem well able to keep themselves occupied while their husbands are at work,' he told her.

'Most wives are not incarcerated in a foreign country,' she reminded him bitterly.

He pushed his chair back from his desk in an abrupt gesture that startled her. 'Let's go.'

Celena frowned. 'Where?'

'To Palermo—where else? Are you ready?'

'I'm not asking you to come with me,' she said. 'Besides, it will be no fun if you're in this mood; I'd rather go alone.'

'And I would rather we went together,' he barked.

With a mental shrug Celena fetched her bag, and in less than ten minutes they were on their way.

Palermo was noisy with traffic and crowded with people but she loved it. Had she gone on her own she would have found it impossible to park, and would probably have got hopelessly lost, and so was thankful, in some degree, for Luc insisting he accompany her.

To have done the capital justice it would have been necessary to stay at least a week, and in just a few hours they no more than scratched the surface. It was oppressively hot as they jostled with swarms of people in the Byzantine street markets, and Celena exclaimed over the latest Milanese fashions displayed in shops that were almost hidden between Renaissance churches and Spanish palaces.

When one particular dress caught her eye Luc insisted that she go inside and try it on, and, parading before him in the peacock-hued silk, Celena felt a stirring of her senses.

For the last few days, since the night they had met Simone and Raimondo in the restaurant, he had been quite cool towards her; now there was a gleam of hunger in his eyes. Admittedly the dress showed her figure to its best advantage, emphasising the pertness of her breasts and the narrowness of her waist, and the slit in the straight skirt revealed a tantalising amount of thigh when she moved.

And seeing his need of her made Celena hungry for him too, and he saw it in her eyes and for a brief moment no one else existed except the two of them. It

was a magical, tangible thing and completely broke
down any reservations she felt.

'You're ravishing, Celena,' he muttered, finally shat-
tering the silence, and to the hovering assistant he said,
'We'll take it.' Outside in the street he announced
thickly, 'If you've seen enough we'll go.'

She knew what was on his mind and it was on hers
too. Despite the fact that she had married him for all
the wrong reasons there was no denying the magnetic
attraction. It was too strong for either of them, and in
the car she could actually feel the pull of him, feel
herself gravitating towards him, and when he rested his
hand on her thigh it was even worse.

Neither spoke—they did not need to—and he drove
with an urgency that suited her mood. All she could
think of was the feel of his hard body against her, the
exquisite rapture of shared pleasure. And the sooner
the better.

The long drive seemed even longer because of her
aching need. It was a peculiar feeling to want a man so
badly, especially someone who did not love her. It had
never happened before; she actually did not believe in
sex without love, sex for the sake of sex, but, dear Lord,
she wanted Luc at this moment, even half prayed that
he would pull off the road somewhere so that they
could satiate their mutual hunger without further delay.

Eventually they reached the house and entered hand
in hand, but before they had reached the privacy of
their rooms Francesca waylaid them. 'Excuse me,
signore, but your great-grandmother is asking for you.
She says it is very urgent.'

'Do you know what it is about?' Luc asked with a
sharp frown.

'Her solicitor came this morning; I think it is something to do with her will,' answered the girl. 'Though
I'm not sure that I should be telling you.'

'No, that's all right,' Luciano assured her, but Celena had already sensed the change in him. All desire had gone, he had become suddenly agitated—and it was not difficult to guess the reason why. If Giacoma made any changes affecting his future then all this would have been for nothing.

CHAPTER TWELVE

THE minutes dragged as Celena waited for Luc. He was certainly a long time in talking to his great-grandmother and she could not help wondering whether her future was about to be drastically changed.

It was quite feasible that she would be sent back to England if Luc discovered that he was not getting his inheritance after all. Lord, he would be angry. It was his main aim in life—so much so that he had entered into a loveless marriage simply to make sure that he would become head of the Segurini family.

When he did return his face was grim and he volunteered nothing, and nor did Celena feel that she was in any position to ask. If he wanted her to leave he would tell her soon enough. He shut himself in his office and she spent the evening alone, going to bed early, though she was still wide awake when Luc came up.

He took a shower then climbed into bed and Celena sensed the tenseness in him. He lay still and straight with his back to her and she ached to touch him but somehow did not dare.

The next morning when she awoke the bed beside her was empty and it matched the empty feeling in her heart. Although she had always known that she was being used it hurt that Luc was shutting her out so absolutely now. Couldn't he have at least told her what Giacoma had wanted?

Whenever Luc went to England Celena paid the old lady a daily visit, but when he was at home and dutifully went to see her himself she did not always bother.

Today, though, she decided she *would* go and see his great-grandmother. Perhaps she would learn something of what had gone on.

She had no idea where her husband was—both the kitchen and his office were empty—and she ate a solitary breakfast before making her way up to Giacoma's rooms. Her tap on the door was answered by the customary, *'Avanti!'* and Celena entered nervously.

'My dear child, how nice of you to come and see me. I was asking Luciano only the other day why you never came any more.' The old lady looked pale and frail this morning, her rings heavy on her fingers.

Celena sat down and looked at the woman concernedly. 'I am sorry, I—'

'My great-grandson keeps you busy, I know,' Giacoma interrupted gently. 'Do not fret. He is a great worker and thinks everyone should be the same. I am so pleased he has decided to make this his permanent home. Are you happy here, my child?'

Celena nodded but the woman was not deceived. 'There is something wrong—I can see it in your eyes. You must tell me what it is. Is Luciano paying more attention to his work than to you—is that it? I know how much it means to him, but he must—'

'Please,' insisted Celena, 'it is not that. He took me to Palermo yesterday; I had a wonderful time.'

'Then why do you look so troubled?'

Celena searched quickly for an excuse. 'It is you I am worried about, Bisnonna. You do not look well this morning.'

'Nonsense, child,' said the old woman at once. 'But thank you for your concern. Where is Luciano now? He hasn't been to see me this morning.'

Celena shrugged. 'I'm not sure; he'd already gone out when I awoke. I expect it's business that's taken

him somewhere.' Or Simone! For all she knew he could
have left her bed in the middle of the night and gone to
the other woman. The thought brought a nasty taste to
her mouth, but it was certainly a possibility—especially
if Giacoma had changed her will and she, Celena, was
of no further use to him. It was obvious that he would
go to the girl he was in love with for solace.

She stayed for a quarter of an hour but Giacoma
dropped no hints as to what she had wanted to see
Luciano about, and finally Celena left, feeling, if possible, even more saddened than she had earlier.

When Luc did eventually return he went straight to
his office, and when Celena asked where he had been
he looked at her as though she was a stranger. 'I don't
have to explain all of my moves to you.'

Tears pricked the backs of her eyelids but she turned
on her heel and left before he could see her distress;
and in the days that followed, when Luciano continued
to remain distant, she knew that the time had come for
her to leave; she could not go on like this any longer.

Biding her time, she made a thorough search for her
passport, but to no avail. She guessed that he had it
locked in a safe somewhere. Not that she need necess-
arily go back to England; she could go to Italy; she
would arrange to have money sent out of her account
to wherever she decided to stay.

Her mind made up, Celena spent a few more days
plotting and planning, and, as though the fates were
looking after her, on the day she decided to leave Luc
told her that he was going to see the managing director
of the car company. 'I need to iron out a problem with
their advertising campaign; I'll probably be gone the
whole day. If anything urgent comes through from
London you know where you can get in touch with me.'

Celena nodded.

'And give my apologies to Bisnonna. Tell her that

I'll be in to see her this evening. And again, you know where I am if she—' He stopped and shook his head, a curious pain in his eyes.

If she what? thought Celena. Changed her mind about her will? It was a curious state of affairs and the sooner she got away from here the better. Hanging around loving a man who had lost all interest in her was causing her nothing but heartache. She could not think why Luc hadn't sent her back home before now. No, that was wrong—she did know why. He didn't want to lose face with his great-grandmother.

But her mind was made up and once Luc had gone she packed her suitcase and tugged off her rings, which she left on the dresser, beside the box with the diamond necklace. There was no need to leave a message; Luc would know exactly what it meant.

As soon as Francesca was safely closeted with Giacoma Celena let herself out of the house. She had decided to hire a car and drive herself up to Messina in the north-east where she would take a ferry across to Italy. From there she would lose herself somewhere in the countryside where Luc could not have a hope of finding her.

As her case was too heavy to carry all the way into Enna she hid it in a hedgerow a little way from the house, planning to pick it up once she had a car.

To her dismay she bumped into Raimondo once she was in town. 'Celena.' He looked pleased to see her. 'You're looking very determined this morning. Where are you off to?'

She shrugged and gave a weak smile. 'Nowhere really, just taking a walk.'

'Then you won't mind if I join you?'

Celena let him fall into step beside her, hoping he wouldn't take up too much of her time. 'How is your friendship with Simone progressing?' she asked, by way of making conversation.

He pulled his mouth wryly down at the corners. 'She's a bit too full of herself for me to take any serious interest. Although she looks amazingly like you—and it's true I did mistake her for you—she has none of your ways. She seems very fond of Luciano, however.' His eyes narrowed and he looked at her questioningly. 'I understand they were once very close.'

'It's all over now,' said Celena airily. It would be improper to air her grievances to this man. If she wanted her plan to succeed she could not risk his guessing her intent. She had to pretend that there was absolutely nothing wrong.

'Are you happy in your marriage, Celena?'

The unexpected question surprised her and she looked at him sharply. 'What makes you ask?'

'Whenever I see you,' he said, 'you always look hauntingly sad, not how I imagine a new bride to be. Perhaps it is Simone who bothers you? I think you know as well as I do that she is still in love with Luciano and does not care who sees it. It is a pity, and the girl ought to be put in her place. Luciano doesn't care for her, I can tell that; he has eyes only for you.'

Eyes only for her! He was the second person to say that. How Celena would have loved to tell him the truth—the whole truth—but all she could do was smile feebly.

'I confess I wouldn't mind being in his shoes,' he went on. 'If I had met you first I—'

Warm colour flooded Celena's cheeks as she looked at him in shock, and Raimondo immediately stopped. 'I am sorry, I should not have said that. It was entirely out of order, even if it is the truth. I think it would be best if I let you proceed with your walk.'

Ruefully he turned back and Celena drew in an

unsteady breath before carrying on. It had never
occurred to her that Raimondo was attracted to her;
she had simply thought he was being kind. She was glad
that she had not known. There were enough compli-
cations in her life without Raimondo adding to them.

After hiring a car in her maiden name Celena drove
warily back through the village, mentally crossing her
fingers that Raimondo would not spot her. Luck was
with her and she was able to pick up her luggage and
head away from the *palazzo* without any mishap.

Armed with a map of Sicily, she headed north over
the mountains, concentrating on the unfamiliar roads,
wryly conscious of the fact that she was unable to
appreciate the grandeur of its dramatic scenery.

With every kilometre that passed she felt a growing
sense of release; although she loved Luc quite desperately she could not handle the situation he had put her
in. What had started out as an exciting new job had
turned into purgatory.

Celena had almost reached Messina when a tyre blew
as she rounded a particularly hazardous bend. The
other side of the road dropped away steeply and no
matter how she struggled with the wheel Celena was
unable to stop the car from going into a terrifying skid.
She closed her eyes in horror as she realised what was
about to happen.

Sicily had a beautiful rugged coastline which she was
suddenly experiencing at close range! The car rolled
over and over as it plummeted, and Celena felt every
bump on the way—it was almost like a replay of her
dream, though there was no Luc to save her this time.

She had visions of the vehicle bursting into flames
when it reached the bottom—cars always did in films—
and knew that she had to be prepared to get out
quickly—if she was still alive!

Struggling to reach the release on the seatbelt, she

somehow never made it, blacking out before the car shuddered to a halt, and when she woke up she was in a hospital bed.

What had happened to cause the pain that attacked every part of her she did not know.

A pretty young nurse looked relieved that she had gained consciousness. 'I will fetch the doctor,' she said. 'He asked to be told the second you came round.'

The doctor was middle-aged and rotund and came hurrying into the ward a few minutes later, smiling kindly at her. 'Welcome back to the land of the living.'

Celena frowned, feeling completely disorientated. 'Where am I? Why do I hurt so much?'

'You had an accident,' he told her gently. 'As a matter of fact you're very lucky to be alive.'

She closed her eyes. 'I can't remember what happened. I can't remember any of it.'

'It is the body's way of dealing with trauma,' said the doctor reassuringly. 'Do not worry; it will come back to you when you're stronger. Our main concern at the moment is to let your family know where you are. I'm afraid we don't even know your name.'

'Lena Coulsden,' she said.

'And your address?'

'Number three, Fountain Mews, Bedrock Road, Chelsea.'

The doctor frowned. 'Where is that?'

'Why, London, of course.' Then it suddenly occurred to Celena that she was not speaking in English, that she had automatically answered the Latin-looking doctor in his own language. 'Where am I?' she enquired.

'You're in Sicily,' he told her quietly.

'Sicily?' she asked in panic.

'It is all right.' He put a reassuring hand over hers.

'No, it is not all right,' she insisted. 'What am I doing in a foreign country?'

'I do not know, I am afraid,' he answered with a wry smile. 'We will have to be patient and let nature take its course. Meanwhile I can assure you that you are in very good hands.'

'But I can't be in Sicily!' she exclaimed. 'I don't know anyone here. Where is my handbag? I must have—' The exertion suddenly became too much for her; her eyes closed and she drifted back into a troubled sleep.

During the next twenty-four hours Celena faded in and out of consciousness, desperately trying to remember, feeling no reassurance when the doctor told her that temporary amnesia was normal.

She had vivid, disturbing dreams of being in prison, though she was never able to find out what she had done, and then one day she opened her eyes to find a complete stranger sitting beside her bed. A very physical man with shiny jet-black hair, side-parted and swept back off his face, he had a square chin and hollow cheeks and looked as though he hadn't slept for days. Another doctor? she wondered. A specialist come to take a look at her?

He smiled gently and took her hand. 'Celena, thank goodness you're awake at last. How are you?'

Celena! No one ever called her Celena, and he was speaking in English! She frowned faintly. 'I still hurt and ache in all the same places,' she answered, puzzled. 'How much longer is it going to take me to get better?'

To her amazement he began stroking her hand, and then he leaned forward and would have kissed her had she not jerked away in horror.

'I'm sorry,' he said. 'I shouldn't have done that. The doctor warned me that you had a temporary memory loss. I just thought that if I—'

'You're damn right you shouldn't have done it,' she

said explosively. 'Who the devil are you? What gives you the right to go around molesting patients?'

He looked desperately saddened by her outburst. 'Celena, I know you don't remember this, but you are my wife.'

'Your wife?' she shrieked, her eyes going down to her ringless fingers. 'I think you're fooling yourself, mister. I would certainly remember if I was married to you.' If only for the reason that she found him physically exciting—despite her injuries, despite his shocking behaviour.

'I can assure you that we are married, Celena,' he said quietly.

She looked into his eyes—beautiful velvet-brown eyes—and felt her stomach curling into knots. 'I would remember,' she insisted firmly. Who could possibly forget this handsome specimen of manhood?

'You do not remember the accident; you do not know why you are in Sicily,' he reminded her sadly, still holding her hands in his. 'Therefore it is perfectly conceivable that you do not remember me.'

'On that reckoning any man could come up and say he was my husband,' Celena declared. 'Why aren't I wearing a ring if I am married?'

'I have it here,' he told her, producing a box from his pocket. 'Will you put it on for me?' he asked softly.

Celena firmly shook her head. 'It doesn't make sense. Why have *you* got the ring? Why isn't it here on my finger? I think you're a fraud, Mr Whoever-you-are.'

'Luciano Segurini,' he told her, his eyes both hurt and pleading at the same time.

The name meant nothing to her. 'How long have we been married—*if* we are?'

'One month.'

'And we live here in Sicily?'

'That's right.'

'What's happened to my mews house in Chelsea?'

'It's up for sale.'

'How did we meet?'

His lips quirked. 'You—came to work for me.'

'What do you do?'

'I run an advertising agency—Luse.'

Celena frowned. 'I'm a copywriter—but I work for Hillier and Jones, not Luse. I've heard of the firm, but. . .'

'It all happened very quickly,' he told her.

She shook her head then stopped because it hurt. She had multiple injuries, mainly broken bones and bruising, nothing as serious as they had first thought, but she was nevertheless in a great deal of discomfort, with her left leg and both arms in plaster, and stitches across her forehead.

'But Luse is in London; why are we—you living here?'

'It is my family home.'

Celena had a sudden flash in her mind's eye of a decaying palace set in beautiful, wooded country high on a mountainside, and then it went again just as quickly. 'What is it like?'

'It's—quite a big place, I suppose.'

'In a town?'

He shook his head. 'No—near Enna, on a mountain with marvellous views. It's magnificent.'

'And do we live there alone?'

He smiled faintly. 'Not exactly, though we do have our own rooms. Over the years it has been divided into several different apartments in which various members of my family live. We can go about our own business without seeing each other for weeks.'

'Like the royal family in London?' she asked quizzically.

'I guess so,' he agreed.

Another picture—of an old lady with button-bright eyes. She searched her mind. 'Does your—er—grandmother live there?'

'My great-grandmother,' he corrected her. 'Do you remember her? Giacoma. She is very fond of you, and desperately worried about you now. She blames herself.'

Celena frowned. 'For what?'

'Making you so unhappy that you ran away.'

'I ran away,' queried Celena, wide-eyed, 'after just one month of marriage?'

Luc's lips twisted wretchedly and he nodded.

'And it was—Giacoma's fault?'

He shook his head. 'No, definitely not. It was my fault you ran away—mine entirely. I've been distrusting and neglectful, and I hate myself for it.' He leaned closer, his pleading brown eyes on hers. 'Darling Celena, I love you so much; I can't bear the thought of life without you. As soon as you're better I want you to come home; I promise—'

Celena stopped listening, wondering why it made her feel good when he said he loved her. She studied his face—the deeply chiselled jaw and cheekbones, the straight nose, slightly flared at the tip, thick, jutting brows over wonderfully sexy eyes. She lay back against the pillows; it was all too much for her.

'You're tired,' he said at once. 'I've been talking too much. I'll go, let you get some sleep.' He kissed a finger and touched it to her lips. 'Remember, I love you.'

Celena slept, and in her dreams she saw Luc clearly; she saw the *palazzo* and Giacoma, she saw his brothers and sister, Filippo and Paolo and Gabriella—and then she saw Simone—and she remembered—and she woke up in a sweat.

The swine! He did not love her, he loved this other woman. He had married her simply because he wanted to be head of the Segurini family. But something had happened—she frowned as she struggled to remember. Giacoma had changed her will—and he had been very distant towards her, Celena, after that. She had been unable to cope and had run away—hired a car—skidded off the road—rolled down a cliff. She remembered no more of the accident.

The doctor came, pleased with her progress. 'You are recovering your memory, I believe? Little things are coming back to you?'

She looked at him bitterly. 'It is almost fully recovered, and I don't want my husband here again. I was running away from him; I hate him; keep him away from me, will you?'

The man looked disturbed. 'I'm sure things can't be that bad. He is very concerned.'

'Of course he's damn well concerned,' she snapped. 'But ours isn't an ordinary marriage. He was using me— and I want out of it. I want you to get me back to England before he comes again.'

'I never went away.' Luc came into her line of vision, sadness in his eyes as he looked at her. And then he turned to the doctor. 'Can you leave us alone for a few minutes?'

The doctor shook his head. 'I think that under the circumstances, considering your wife's distress and the fact that she is still a very sick person, it would be best if you left her alone for a while.'

'Like for ever,' intervened Celena hostilely.

But Luc was at his most persuasive, and after talking softly to the doctor for a few minutes the portly man reluctantly left.

Luc sat down beside the bed, his eyes never leaving Celena's face. He looked more gaunt than ever, and abjectly unhappy, and he made no attempt to touch her.

'Talking won't make any difference,' she said flatly.

A muscle jerked fiercely in his jaw. 'Tell me why you couldn't stand me any longer.'

Her eyes flashed. 'Isn't it obvious? Let's face it, Luc, you only married me because if you remained a bachelor you would forfeit your right to become head of your family.'

Shock drew his brows together. 'I thought I had corrected you on that point; you should not listen to idle gossip. It is nonsense. Goodness, I couldn't care less about it.'

'Simone said that's what you wanted.'

He frowned. 'Did she now? Is that who put the idea into your mind? Maybe it was what *she* wanted; she rather fancied the thought of being the *grande madame*. It looks as though I'll have to put that young lady straight.'

Celena still glared. 'Your brother said the same.'

'Filippo?'

She nodded.

'That I do not understand,' he said, his frown deepening until it carved a deep groove in his brow.

'He said you always had to be top dog, even when you were children.'

Luc laughed then, though uneasily. 'It's true, but only in the way boys compete. I never told him that being head of the family was more important than anything else. Heavens, Celena, you matter to me more than anything else in the whole world. I meant it when I said I love you; I can't face the thought of life without you.'

Her chin lifted, her eyes still distrustful, even though her heart had leapt almost out of her ribcage. 'You had a funny way of showing it.'

He grimaced. 'Because I was scared.'

She frowned. Luc scared? It did not make sense. 'Of what?'

'I couldn't bear the thought of you laughing in my face, of it being one-sided. I just hoped that one day, if I could keep you with me long enough, you would learn to love me too.'

Celene's eyes were still hard. 'How do I know that you're speaking the truth? How do I know that it's not still a pack of lies designed to keep me at your side? You've never been open with me.'

'I know,' he agreed sadly, 'but I couldn't take the risk that you wouldn't agree to help me out. I had to play it the way I did. The truth is, Celena, that I was strongly attracted to you the very first time I saw you at that convention.'

She frowned. 'But you were going out with Simone then.'

'I know,' he admitted ruefully. 'That's what makes it all the more incredible. I think, though, that I'd actually begun to realise even then that Simone wasn't the perfect girl I thought she was. But it wasn't until she left me that I remembered the extraordinary likeness between you and realised that you could help me out of a delicate situation.'

'So you planned right from the beginning to marry me!' she accused hostilely.

'Goodness, no!' he exclaimed. 'That was inspiration, once I discovered that I'd fallen in love with you. Although my *bisnonna* dearly wanted to see me married she would never have wished me to do so just to make her happy. The engagement was planned, I'll admit, but only because they were expecting it.'

'You could have played the wedding part straight,' she chided. 'You must have known that I felt an attraction too.'

'A physical one,' he admitted ruefully, 'but that wasn't enough. There were times when I thought it was; then I realised what a selfish bastard I was being.'

Celena closed her eyes for a moment, her love for Luc welling up and threatening to choke her. But there were still many things to be sorted before she could open her own heart. 'How about Simone now?'

He pulled a face. 'She is a problem, I confess, but I think she has finally got the message. I was out of my mind when you disappeared without trace; she would have had to be blind not to see how much I loved you.'

'You sometimes gave me the impression that you loved *her*.'

Again a rueful grimace. 'To try and make you jealous, my sweet, though I realise now that it is impossible to make someone jealous if she does not love you in the first place.' He dragged in a heavy, regretful breath.

Celena changed the subject. 'How *did* you manage to track me down? Apparently I had no identification on me. I don't know what happened to my stuff.'

'Burnt,' he announced tersely. 'The car caught fire— everything went. Mercifully you were thrown clear; you obviously hadn't fastened your seat belt.' He shuddered as he spoke and dropped his head in his hands, and Celena knew then for certain that he loved her.

There was torture on his face when he looked at her again, torment in his eyes. 'When I got back home and found you missing, and your wedding ring on the dresser, I went out of my mind. All along I had been so terrified that you would leave; I knew you weren't happy, and yet I had this vain hope that if I kept you long enough you would one day learn to love me. It's why I took your passport and everything else, why I wouldn't let you go back to England—just in case you refused to return.'

'And why you insisted I remain a prisoner in the house?' she asked bitterly.

'No,' he said at once, 'not that. I know it must have

been awful for you, and I'm extremely sorry for the distress I caused, but there was a very good reason.'

Celena raised her brows and waited.

'You remember when I said there was a danger of you being kidnapped?'

She nodded. 'I didn't believe you for one minute.'

'You should have done,' he said sadly. 'I didn't want to alarm you too much by going into detail but the truth is that there have been several such attacks on wealthy families recently. I couldn't take the risk of it happening to you; you were too precious. It is also why my great-grandmother insisted on her hairdresser and everyone else coming to you.'

'You should have been more insistent,' Celena reproved him, feeling a faint shudder down her spine. 'You should have told me everything. I left myself wide open every time I went into Enna.'

He nodded grimly. 'The good news is that I heard on the radio only yesterday that the offenders have been caught—otherwise I would have assumed that that's what had happened to you.' He groaned at the very idea.

Celena found it difficult to breathe; her eyes never left his face.

'As it was, especially when I saw the ring, I knew you had simply run away. I didn't know what to do. I rang all the airports, the ferries—everywhere I could think of. Nothing. No one fitting your description had been seen. I decided you must still be in Sicily. Buses and taxis—I drew a blank. Car hire? No. Raimondo? Jealousy flared. That was it—you had run away with Raimondo. I went to his establishment, not expecting to find him there, relieved in one way when I did, but disturbed when he said that he thought he had seen you driving through Enna. He said he had been talking to you earlier and you had looked desperately unhappy.'

Raimondo had seen her after all!

'I then discovered that you had hired a car in Enna under your maiden name, Coulsen, using the dimunitive, Lena, as your first name. Very clever, Celena.'

She shrugged. 'There was nothing clever about it; my driving licence hadn't been changed. And it's only you who calls me Celena.'

'Your driving licence!' he exclaimed. 'I missed that. But, to carry on—while I was in the car-hire office they had a telephone call to say that one of their cars had been found burnt out.' His teeth clenched, muscles contracted in his jaw. 'The car you had hired!' His eyes were stricken as he looked at her. 'I really thought I had lost you.' Tears welled now. 'Darling Celena, what had I done? I had driven you to your death.' He checked a sob. 'I wanted to die too.'

Tears now raced down Celena's cheeks. 'Oh, Luc.' There was no escaping the fact now that he truly did love her. 'Luc! I am so sorry.'

He bowed his head again, wanting to hide from her his distress. 'I'm the one who should be apologising. Of course you're free to go. I realise now that it was wrong of me to—'

'Luc,' she interrupted softly, 'I don't want to go. I love you.'

He stilled and she knew that he was questioning whether he had heard her correctly.

'I love you, Luc,' she repeated.

He looked up then and she saw the shimmering shape of him through her tears, and his eyes were misted too. And she wanted to throw her arms around him but couldn't because of the plaster casts.

'Celena?' he asked thickly.

'It is true,' she told him.

'But—' he frowned '—I don't understand. Why were you going if—?'

'Because I thought you loved Simone, because I thought you were using me, because I thought you'd get rid of me anyway once I'd served my purpose, because of a thousand and one stupid reasons,' she said in a rush. 'Oh, Luc!'

'Celena.' He came to her then, holding her very gently, very carefully, and his lips brushed hers, checking with difficulty the passion and hunger that was rising inside him.

The doctor looked in and went away again with a quiet smile, and neither of them saw him.

'If only you'd been honest,' she said, 'it would have saved us both this heartache. You didn't have to do anything so drastic as marrying me.'

'I wanted you,' he said thickly, and his mouth closed over hers again.

The power of love, she thought happily.

'Can I safely assume that ours will now be a proper marriage?' he asked at length.

Shyly Celena nodded.

'I want a family,' he said. 'A large one. I want our house filled with laughing voices. Does that horrify you?'

She smiled. 'Not in the least, and think how happy Giacoma will be.'

He looked sad all of a sudden and sat back in his chair, though he still held her hands. 'Giacoma is dying.'

Celena felt his distress.

'Her doctor has not given her much longer to live; I don't think she will make it to our first child. She is refusing to go into hospital and be operated on, says she has had a long run and is happy to step down and let me take her place.' He shook his head as he spoke. 'It is the last thing I want, I love her so much. She has been both a mother and father to me; she is an incredibly wise old lady. And she loves you too, Celena—dearly, as if you were her own.'

'I love her also,' Celena admitted.

'She's changed her will—do you know that?—to include you in it. You certainly made a good impression on her.'

Celena frowned. 'Was that what she wanted to see you about the other day?'

He nodded.

'But you were so distant afterwards,' she said with a frown. 'I thought it was because she was disinheriting you. I thought you weren't going to get your wish to become head of the family. I thought that's why you suddenly withdrew from me.' She twisted her lips ruefully. 'It's the main reason I ran away.'

'Oh, Celena,' he groaned, 'it was because I was totally distressed. I went to see her doctor myself but he could give me no hope. I blindly thought she would live for ever; she always gave that impression. I shall miss her, Celena. Thank God I've got you.'

'For always,' she murmured, hating to see this man of hers so sad. It was this caring side of him that she liked; she had always abhorred the thought that he was mercenary. How glad she was that she had been proved wrong.

'And for always I will love you and look after you,' he promised. 'No more secrets, no more hiding the truth. I love you, Celena Segurini, from the bottom of my heart. And if you don't want to live in the family home, then we will find somewhere—'

'No,' interjected Celena firmly. 'I love it.'

He frowned. 'But you've shown no interest.'

'Only because I thought I would be shipped back to England. What was the point, I asked myself, when I wouldn't reap the benefit? Now it is different; I shall throw myself into it wholeheartedly while you look after Luse.'

'Don't tire yourself out,' he warned. 'I don't want a wife who goes to sleep on me every night.'

'As if I would,' she laughed. 'By the time this lot's off—' she indicated the plaster casts '—we shall have a lot of catching up to do, and I for one intend to take every advantage of you.'

He grinned. 'That's what I like—a woman who knows her own mind.'

'I've known it a long time,' she admitted. 'It's why you were able to hurt me so much. You're a remarkable man, Luciano Segurini. One look at you and I was hooked.'

'It's obvious we were made for each other,' he said with a satisfied smile.

'Without a doubt,' she confirmed.

'And we would have found each other one day even if I hadn't forced the issue.'

'I'm sure of it,' she agreed.

'I love you so very much, Celena. My heart would have broken in two if I'd lost you. I am so, so sorry to have caused you such anguish.'

'Shh,' she whispered fiercely. 'No more apologies, no more regrets. We've found each other, we love each other—that is enough.'

'You are my life.' His eyes filled with tears again.

'And you are mine,' she said, a lump rising in her throat. And as they kissed their tears merged and they tasted the salt of them, and it was the beginning of their new life together.

MILLS & BOON®

Next Month's Romances

♡

Each month you can choose from a wide variety of romance with Mills & Boon. Below are the new titles to look out for next month in our two new series Presents and Enchanted.

Presents™

TOO WISE TO WED?	Penny Jordan
GOLD RING OF BETRAYAL	Michelle Reid
THE SECOND MRS ADAMS	Sandra Marton
HONEYMOON FOR THREE	Sandra Field
THE UNEXPECTED FATHER	Kathryn Ross
RYAN'S RULES	Alison Kelly
SUBSTITUTE BRIDE	Angela Devine
THE DOMINANT MALE	Sarah Holland

Enchanted™

BRINGING UP BABIES	Emma Goldrick
FALLING FOR HIM	Debbie Macomber
SECOND-BEST WIFE	Rebecca Winters
THE BABY BATTLE	Shannon Waverly
HIS CINDERELLA BRIDE	Heather Allison
MISLEADING ENGAGEMENT	Marjorie Lewty
A ROYAL ROMANCE	Valerie Parv
LIVING WITH MARC	Jane Donnelly

GET 4 BOOKS
AND A MYSTERY GIFT

Return this coupon and we'll send you 4 Mills & Boon Presents™ novels and a mystery gift absolutely FREE! We'll even pay the postage and packing for you.

We're making you this offer to introduce you to the benefits of Reader Service: FREE home delivery of brand-new Mills & Boon Presents novels, at least a month before they are available in the shops, FREE gifts and a monthly Newsletter packed with information.

Accepting these FREE books and gift places you under no obligation to buy, you may cancel at any time, even after receiving just your free shipment. Simply complete the coupon below and send it to:

MILLS & BOON® READER SERVICE, FREEPOST, CROYDON, SURREY, CR9 3WZ.

No stamp needed

Yes, please send me 4 free Mills & Boon Presents novels and a mystery gift. I understand that unless you hear from me, I will receive 6 superb new titles every month for just £2.10* each, postage and packing free. I am under no obligation to purchase any books and I may cancel or suspend my subscription at any time, but the free books and gift will be mine to keep in any case. (I am over 18 years of age)

P6LE

Ms/Mrs/Miss/Mr _____

Address _____

_____

_____ Postcode _____

Offer closes 30th June 1997. We reserve the right to refuse an application. *Prices and terms subject to change without notice. Offer only valid in UK and Ireland and is not available to current subscribers to this series. **Readers in Ireland please write** to: P.O. Box 4546, Dublin 24. Overseas readers please write for details.

You may be mailed with offers from other reputable companies as a result of this application. Please tick box if you would prefer not to receive such offers. ☐